HC

Brice had removed his chainmail and the other accoutrements of fighting and war and stood there as just a man. Yet now he seemed even more dangerous than before.

He was tall and large, with broad shoulders that spoke of years of training in his craft. She swallowed deeply as she realised he watched her perusal of him. Gillian lowered her gaze to her clasped hands and waited quietly. Without even lifting her head, she could see him moving closer to her.

'Do you need something to drink or eat?'

'My lord,' she said quietly as she rose to her feet and stood before him, 'I need nothing from you save your grant of safe passage to the convent.'

The tension between and around them grew as she waited on his word. His brown eyes darkened even more as the intensity and heat of his gaze moved over her.

'You have asked for one of the two things I could not grant you, lady, even if I wished it to be so.'

Her heart began to pound in her chest as he reached out and took her hand in his, tugging her even closer.

'What is the other?' She held her breath as he lifted her hand to his mouth and kissed the inside of her wrist. He allowed his lips to rest there for a moment longer than necessary before looking back at her.

'I could not let you greet the morning as a maiden still.'

Terri Brisbin is wife to one, mother of three and dental hygienist to hundreds when not living the life of a glamorous romance author. She was born, raised and is still living in the southern New Jersey suburbs. Terri's love of history led her to write time-travel romances and historical romances set in Scotland and England. Readers are invited to visit her website for more information at www.terribrisbin.com, or contact her at PO Box 41, Berlin, NJ 08009-0041, USA.

Previous novels by the same author:

THE DUMONT BRIDE
LOVE AT FIRST STEP
   (short story in *The Christmas Visit*)
THE NORMAN'S BRIDE
THE COUNTESS BRIDE
THE EARL'S SECRET
TAMING THE HIGHLANDER
SURRENDER TO THE HIGHLANDER
POSSESSED BY THE HIGHLANDER
BLAME IT ON THE MISTLETOE
   (short story in *One Candlelit Christmas*)
THE MAID OF LORNE
THE CONQUEROR'S LADY*

and in Mills & Boon® Historical *Undone!* eBooks:

A NIGHT FOR HER PLEASURE*

*The Knights of Brittany

Soren's story is next in Terri Brisbin's
The Knights of Brittany
Look for
HIS ENEMY'S DAUGHTER
coming soon in Mills & Boon® Historical

THE MERCENARY'S BRIDE

Terri Brisbin

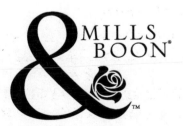

First published in Great Britain 2011
by Mills & Boon, an imprint of Harlequin (UK) Limited,
Eton House, 18-24 Paradise Road, Richmond, Surrey TW9 1SR

© Theresa S. Brisbin 2010

ISBN: 978 0 263 22281 4

Harlequin (UK) policy is to use papers that are natural, renewable and recyclable products and made from wood grown in sustainable forests. The logging and manufacturing process conform to the legal environmental regulations of the country of origin.

Printed and bound in Great Britain
by CPI Antony Rowe, Chippenham, Wiltshire

THE MERCENARY'S BRIDE

Prologue

Taerford Manor, Wessex, England
December 1066

Bishop Obert summoned a meeting with the second of the knights on the list he'd prepared months before of those who were to benefit from the king's generosity. He carried the papers with him that would turn the knight into a baron and make a penniless bastard into a rich lord—if he could take the lands granted him from the Saxon rebels who still held them.

Obert paced along the length of the table, waiting for Brice Fitzwilliam, bastard knight from Brittany, to arrive. If he was to make it back to London before the king's coronation he must leave on the morrow, and this was his last duty here in Taerford. Regardless of the winter closing in around them, regardless of the yet unsettled lands and regardless of his own wants or needs, he was Duke William's loyal servant. After God, of course, he mused as he turned towards the group of men now approaching.

As seemed to be their custom, the new lord of Taerford,

Giles Fitzhenry, walked side by side with the man for whom Obert waited. Thinking back to his weeks here, he rarely saw one without the other, whether in the hall or yards, in any task needed to be done here in Taerford. They strode in, followed by more of Giles's men, fresh from practising their fighting skills in the yard. They became quieter with every step closer and bowed as one to him.

'My lord,' he said to Giles first, and then, wishing to proceed with his task, he turned to the other. 'My lord,' he said as he nodded to Fitzwilliam.

The implications were not lost on anyone listening and the hall grew silent as they waited on Obert's words. The surprise filled the warrior's face until he laughed aloud with joy. If it was inappropriate, Obert could understand it—as one bastard pleased by the success of another who shared his status. The ripples of cheering and shouting ebbed quickly as the entire hall watched and waited on the declaration.

Obert motioned the knight forwards to kneel in front of him. Although this should have been more ceremonial and formal, and before the duke himself, the dangers of the times and place gave way to expediency. Lord Giles stood, once more, at his friend's side, placing his hand on Brice's shoulder as Obert continued.

'In the Duke's name, I declare you, Brice Fitzwilliam, now Baron and Lord of Thaxted, and vassal to the Duke himself,' Obert intoned. The pledging of loyalty directly to the duke, who was soon to be king, ensured a network of warriors who owed their lands and titles and wealth to only him, with no other liege lords between them. Obert could not fight the smile that threatened, for it had been his idea to do so. 'As such, you have the right to lay claim to all the lands, the livestock, the villeins and other properties owned or held by the traitor Eoforwic of Thaxted before his death.'

Although the Normans and Bretons present cheered, the peasants who'd lived on this land and claimed Saxon heritage did not. He understood that the victors in any engagement deserved everything they fought so hard to gain, but the compassionate part of him also understood the shame of being the defeated. However, this day belonged to the victorious Breton knight before him.

'The Duke declares that you should marry the daughter of Eoforwic, if possible, or seek another appropriate bride from the surrounding lands and loyal vassals if not.'

Obert handed the new lord the package of folded parchments that carried the grant of lands and titles. Holding out his hands, he waited for Brice to offer his pledge. In a deep voice that shook from the power of this promise, Brice repeated the words as Obert's clerk whispered them.

'By the Lord before whom I, Brice Fitzwilliam, now of Thaxted, swear this oath and in the name of all that is holy, I will pledge to William of Normandy, Duke and now King of all England, to be true and faithful, and to love all which he loves and to shun all which he shuns, according to the laws of God and the order of the world. I swear that I will not ever, with will or action, through word or deed or omission, do anything which is unpleasing to him, on condition that he will hold to me as I shall deserve it, and that he will perform everything as it was in our agreement when I first submitted myself to him and his mercy and chose his will over mine. I offer this unconditionally, with no expectations other than his faith and favour as my liege lord.'

Obert raised his voice so that all could hear.

'I, Obert of Caen, speaking in the name and with the authority of William, Duke of Normandy and King of England, do accept this oath of fealty as sworn here before these witnesses and before God and do promise that William, as lord and king, will protect and defend the person and properties of Brice Fitzwilliam of Thaxted who here pledges on his honour that he will be ruled by the king's will and his word. In the king's name, I agree to the promises contained herein this oath unconditionally, with no expectations other than his faith and service as loyal vassal to the king.'

Obert allowed the words to echo through the hall and then released the new lord of Thaxted to stand before him. 'To Lord Thaxted,' he called out. 'Thaxted!'

The men joined in his cheer then, stamping their feet and clapping their hands and he permitted it to go on for several minutes. Lord Giles pounded his friend on the back and then pulled him into a hug that spoke of years of toil and triumph together. Only when Obert spied Lady Fayth entering the hall did he realise he must speak to Brice about the woman involved. As he watched the expression on the lady's face change several times on her approach after hearing the news of Brice's grant, he knew that the weaker sex had a way of making things difficult for the men chosen or designated to oversee them as lords or husbands.

Obert noticed the hesitation in the lady's greeting and in her congratulatory words even if no one else did. Ah, the soft feelings of women did ever make things more difficult for men. As Lord Giles took her hand and stood by her side, Obert comprehended the biggest difference between the two knights now made lords by their king.

Lord Giles had not had to hunt for his wife once he'd fought his way to his lands.

He could not say the same for Lord Brice.

Chapter One

Thaxted Forest, northeastern England
March 1067

The ground beneath her feet began to shake and Gillian searched for a cause. It was a fair day, considering that winter still claimed the land, but no clouds marred the sky's bright blue expanse. Looking up, she could see no sign of a coming storm that would cause the thunderous noise that covered the area.

Pushing her hood back, Gillian stepped into the road and glanced both ahead and behind. With only a moment to spare, she realised the reason for such a clamour and jumped back into the tangle of brush and bush at the road's edge. With a prayer of thanks offered that she'd stolen a dark brown cloak on her escape, she tugged it around her and lay still as the large group of mounted knights and warriors thundered past her hiding place. When they pulled up a short distance from where she lay motionless and silent, she dared not even breathe for the fear of being detected and captured by these unknown marauders.

Too far away to hear and too low to understand, their words were a jumble of Norman French and some English, as well. Keeping her face down, Gillian waited for them to move on their way. When she heard the sounds of men dismounting and walking along the road, her body began to tremble. Being caught out alone during these dangerous times was an invitation to death or worse and something Gillian had taken pains to avoid.

Her decision to leave her home and flee to the convent was not made in haste or without considering the consequences, but her alternatives were limited and not attractive: the marriage her brother Oremund had arranged to a poxed old man or one the invading duke had made to a vicious Norman warrior on his way to destroy all she held dear. All she could do was stay out of sight and pray this troop of soldiers would move on and her quest to reach the convent would continue.

Gillian waited as the men discussed something and held her breath once more, trying not to gain their attention as their voices grew nearer to the place where she hid. She recognised the name of her home and her brother's, as well. If only they would speak in her tongue or at the least speak slower so that she could try to understand more of their words!

After a few seemingly endless minutes, the men began to walk away from her, calling out to the others that they saw nothing. She raised her head with care as slowly as she could and watched their retreat. But one knight remained in the road, not more than several yards from where she lay. Instead of following the others, he reached up and tugged at his helm, pulling it free and tucking it under his arm as he turned.

The gasp escaped before she could stop it.

He was tall and muscular and the most attractive man she'd

ever beheld, even considering her cousin who was accounted to be every woman's dream. He did not wear his blond hair in the short, shorn Norman-style; instead it hung loosely around his face. She could not tell the colour of his eyes at this distance, but his face was all masculine angles and intriguing in spite of his being a Norman.

A Norman! And a Norman in full battle armour.

Holy Mother of God, protect her!

And he was staring into the trees in her direction. She dared not move, even to seek the cover of the snarls of branches beneath her for he cocked his head, narrowed his eyes and waited. She knew he listened for another sign that someone was hiding and she barely let out her breath as she remained motionless there.

Gillian thought he might come into the thicket to search, but instead he turned to the others before placing his helm on and striding with those long legs back to them. He rained down curses as he walked, some so loud and rude that she felt the heat of a blush creeping up her cheeks. He could not be the lord who the Conqueror had given Thaxted to, for no nobleman would act in such a common way, using words as he had and comparing one of his men to a beast of burden, and a feeble, useless one at that.

So, who was he and what was his mission here?

One of the other men called out orders to move on and she prayed that they would indeed do so. Gillian did not move until the dust settled back on to the road's dry surface and no sounds could be heard. Even then, she dragged herself to sit up and pulled her cloak around her. She would not move from this spot until she was certain that there was a safe and adequate distance between herself and the warriors.

Pulling the skin of watered ale from beneath her cloak, she drank deeply and eased the dryness in her throat. The exertion of walking many miles, the dustiness of the road and the fear that yet pounded in her veins all caused her parched throat and the ale soothed it. Tempted to partake of the food she carried wrapped in cloth, Gillian decided to wait, for she had taken only enough to last her for two days of journeying from the keep to the convent and she had few coins to buy more.

If any at all was available for sale along the way.

The winter had come early and the last harvest was a meagre one, disturbed by plans of wars and their aftermath. Any surplus, even some of that required to feed the number of souls who lived on her father's lands, had gone to feed King Harold's army as it passed close by. They had been first on their way north to face the forces of Harald Hardrada, and then on their way south to battle with the usurper William of Normandy.

King Harold's forces had little chance to regroup after battling the Norse before heading south to meet the Norman forces near the coast. In one short day in mid-September, England's hopes were dashed as her king and many of his closest allies were killed.

Worse, in the months since that battle near Hastings, outlaws and rebels traversed the length of the land seeking what they could take to fuel their efforts against the conquering Norman army. Gillian sighed, her stomach more upset by the memories of these last months and now unable to think about eating. Enough time had passed, she thought, so she stood, brushed the damp soil and leaves from her gown and cloak and made her way to the edge of the road.

Peering up at the sun, she realised she'd most likely lost an hour of precious daylight during this encounter. Stepping on to the road, she increased her previous pace and began her journey anew. She had to reach the convent by sunset or she would spend another night alone in the woods—a thought that scared her more now that she knew these Normans were sharing the road with her.

An hour passed, and then another, and Gillian continued to walk, always with an eye ahead and an ear listening for the sounds of danger, travelling in the same direction as the men while trying to stay far enough behind so that she would never catch up to their pace. As the sun dropped lower in the western sky, she realised she would not make it to the convent before the sisters closed their gates for the night. Surely, she hoped as she wiped the sweat from her brow with the back of her sleeve, sleeping in the shadows of their walls would be nearly as safe as sleeping within them?

She hurried then, deciding to eat the chunk of bread and piece of cheese in her bag and doing so in some haste, slowing only when she reached the rise in the road that signalled she was nearing her destination. Only a few miles separated her from safety. Her breathing grew laboured as she climbed the rising road to its peak and she paused to catch her breath a few times before reaching the summit.

Then she lost the ability to breathe completely as she beheld a terrifying sight—the same troop of warriors, and more now, camped on the side of the road. Gillian glanced ahead and wondered if she could simply continue on her way as though a simple peasant woman on a task. Mayhap they would pay her no mind? Fighting the urge to run, for running now would be nothing less than an invitation to follow her, she decided that a steady pace was her best choice.

Tugging her hood closer over her brow, she lowered her head and put one foot in front of the other, forcing slow, measured steps along the road. Gillian carefully peeked over at the soldiers out of the corner of her eye and hastened her pace past them. Although many approached the road, none stopped her. A quickening of hope beat in her chest as she made her way. She was nearly beyond the camp when a huge man stepped in front of her, blocking her way forwards.

She side-stepped him, or tried to, but he moved as she did. His large size and muscular form spoke of his strength, and Gillian considered her choices. She turned, thinking to go back in the direction from where she'd come, and faced another warrior there. Then a third and fourth man blocked her sides so that she had nowhere to go. Taking and releasing a deep breath, she waited for them to act.

'Mistress, why are you on these roads alone?' one asked in heavily accented English. 'What is your business?'

Although she'd hoped never to need it, Gillian had prepared a story to answer just that question. Without meeting his gaze, she turned to the one who had spoken.

'My lady sends me to the convent, my lord,' she said, hoping that referring to these common soldiers as 'lords' would flatter them and ease her way. She bowed her head lower as she said it.

'The night is almost upon us,' the one at her back said. 'Come, you will be safer in our camp this night.'

Was a sheep safe when guarded by a wolf? She thought not, almost hearing them salivating over her. Shaking her head, she begged off such an invitation. 'The good sisters are expecting me, my lord. I must hasten there now. My lady will be angered if I do not arrive there.'

She pushed against the one in front of her, but he barely moved. Gillian tried once more without success. Before she could try again, two of them grabbed her by her arms and pulled her with them as they walked towards the others. No amount of struggling loosened their iron grips and her heart began to pound in her chest, making her blood pulse and her head spin.

Before she realised it, they were in the middle of the camp, far enough that she could not make an easy escape. She did not make it easy for them, but it neither slowed nor impeded their progress. They simply dragged her between them. Her arms ached from it and she knew her skin would show bruises by morning—if she lived until then.

By their fast and furious whispering amongst themselves, she knew something was wrong. She decided to take advantage of it. Stomping her foot down with all her weight, Gillian pounded on the instep of the one behind her and pushed at him with her hips, trying to force him off balance.

It did not work.

Instead, her own foot now ached from it and she was forced to limp along as they continued forwards. Finally, they stopped and she took advantage of that moment to pull free and run. One soldier grabbed her cloak, which gave way when the laces snapped. Gillian had not taken two steps, two painful steps, before a mail-covered arm wrapped around her waist and dragged her up against the hardest surface she'd ever felt. So hard was it that it knocked the very breath from her lungs and nearly rendered her senseless as her head collided with the top of the chest plate.

'Where are you going now, mistress? Have you decided not to favour us with your presence this night after all?'

When she recognised the voice of the warrior who now held her firmly against him, terror began to tease her senses. With no chance for escape and suspecting that these men were planning all manner of illicit and immoral acts against her, she listened to the laughter of those watching the scene and wished she could faint. Instead, she gasped as the giant behind her wrapped his other arm around her and pulled her into an indecent embrace against his chest. Then he leaned his head closer to hers until she could feel his hot breath against the skin of her neck.

'Tell me what you seek, sweetling,' he whispered in English words flavoured with his exotic foreign accent, 'and I will try to oblige you in any way I can.'

Chapter Two

Though the circumstances and sometimes miserable history of his existence as a bastard among noble-born should have taught him the lesson, Brice Fitzwilliam had never learned the one about patience being a virtue. It had always seemed overrated and a necessary nuisance, and this situation simply confirmed his opinion about it.

After being patient as the king required, and waiting while the winter passed for his letters granting him the lands and titles of Baron and Lord of Thaxted to arrive, he'd made his way here only to find the keep firmly closed against him. Three weeks of waiting for reinforcements from his friend Giles's forces to arrive found him no closer to conquering the keep or the people inside. Now, after capturing a few escaping peasants, he discovered that his bride, who'd run away on several other occasions, had also just escaped under his watch—and that she sought refuge away from his control in a convent. Luckily Stephen le Chasseur accompanied him and nothing and no one escaped him when he set out to hunt.

Though she squirmed in his arms, Brice knew she had no idea of his identity or that she was his. His anger grew for her blithe ignorance of the dangers on the road. If he had not found her, the thought of what could have befallen her terrified him for many reasons. She needed to be taught a lesson and he would be the one to do it.

At least she was alive for him to make her consider her actions.

'So, what is your price for the night, mistress?' he asked, sliding his hand across her body and feeling her shudder beneath his caress. 'Many of my men have saved up their coins or trinkets and could make it worth your while to stay with us.'

'I am not a wh-wh…' she stuttered. 'I do not sell my favours.'

Brice released her and spun her to face him, nearly losing his wits along with it, for he finally got his first clear look at his bride. She was a beauty and she belonged to him.

Wide, luminous eyes, a colour between blue and green, shimmered from a heart-shaped face. Long, dark brown curls escaped from under her veil and tumbled over her shoulders. Though she was dressed in the loose Saxon style, he could see that her body was wonderfully curved and fell into the feminine shape he desired in his lovers—full soft breasts and hips. From the strength of her resistance, he knew that her legs and arms were strong.

His body reacted before his perusal was complete, that part of him flaring to life and readying him for all the things he'd shamelessly threatened her with. Only when one of his men coughed loudly did he speak.

'If not a whore, then what?'

'I told these men that my lady sent me to seek the convent and I am on my way there now.'

'Alone, mistress? When marauders and outlaws of all types roam the woods and control roads here? Surely your lady would have sent along guards to keep you safe?' he asked, stepping closer again.

She backed up, but his men did not and she remained trapped between them. He recognised the growing fear in her gaze and knew her brave front was in danger of crumbling. Then, as he watched, she pulled her confidence together, squared her shoulders and stuck out her chin at him.

'My lady has other things to worry over, sir. She knows that I am self-reliant and could make my own way to the convent.'

Self-reliant? Too much so, for here she was, miles from safety, alone and not for the first time. Foolhardy was more accurate a description, was what he thought right now.

'Foolish?' he asked. 'Seeking trouble?' He let his gaze follow the curves of her body and did not hide his appreciation then. 'Surely, any lady who sends her servant out onto these roads during these…dangerous…times understands the message she is sending.'

Brice could almost hear her trying to swallow her fear. Her eyes shimmered with a hint of tears and her lip, the full lower one that tempted him so much, trembled then. Ah, mayhap she was finally realising the foolishness of her plan?

'A nobleman would honour a lady's promise to her maid and grant her safe passage to the convent. A true nobleman would not take advantage of a woman without protection. A true nobleman would—' She began to list another trait, but he stopped her with a shake of his head.

'I never claimed to be a nobleman, mistress,' he whispered as the anger grew from deep within him. 'If your lady believes that noblemen are to be trusted and would pass up such a temptation as the one you present here, she is more foolish than I first thought.'

His men laughed then, knowing that neither he nor they were of noble or even legitimate birth, and he recognised the confusion in her expression. Most men would have been flattered by her, but not these who had made their way in the world by the work of their labours and the sweat of their bodies.

Lady Gillian looked as though she wanted to argue, but had not the words to do it, so she lowered her head and turned away. His attempts to humiliate her did not give him the satisfaction he'd hoped. Glancing at his men, he knew that nightfall was coming and there were many things that needed to be done now that his bride had walked into his possession.

'Take her to my tent and make sure she stays there,' he ordered.

'You cannot!' she cried out. He stepped closer, forcing her to look up to see his face. 'The good sisters—'

'The good sisters will eat their meal, offer their prayers and seek their beds as they do each night, mistress. Your lady should have thought out her plan before launching it.'

She pushed against him. 'They are expecting me. My lady sent them a message to expect me.'

'I can assure you that no message arrived at the convent. We have been camped here for the last several weeks and no one from Thaxted has crossed our path...until you did this day.'

Her confidence did crumble then and he felt the fight go out of her. She glanced around the camp and for the first time seemed to realise their number and the dangers they presented to her. If there had been a messenger, Brice's men had not seen him. There was every possibility that such a messenger would have fled in the other direction if he'd spied their camp and

knew he could not get through. Apparently, that messenger
did not report his failure to his lady.

'Take her,' he repeated softly and he stepped aside so that
Stephen could carry out his order.

The lady looked as though she would offer resistance, but
she simply nodded and walked off with his men. At least,
praise God, she was safe now and it was one less thing he
needed to worry over in this volatile situation. By morning
she would be his, as would Thaxted Manor and all the lands
entailed to it and to him as Lord of Thaxted.

And with the support of Giles's men from Taerford and some
of the king's forces, Brice would take over the keep, expel the
rebels and those who would not pledge to King William, and
begin his life as one of the high and mighty instead of remaining a low-born soldier. Taking in a deep breath and exhaling
it, Brice knew he looked forwards to much of what yet faced
him in the challenging days ahead.

Facing the lady's fury at his deception was not one of those
things.

Hours passed as he saw to preparations for his final assault against the keep as well as more personal ones involv-
ing the Lady Gillian. He sent word to the convent to let them
know that she was safe and would be returning to her home in
due course. A generous donation accompanied the message,
smoothing, he hoped, the way that future dealings with the
holy sisters would go. He'd watched as many others made the
mistake of not respecting the clergy and he was determined
not to fall into that error himself.

Finally, several hours after the sun dropped into the west
and when night was full upon them, he decided it was time

to take the first step towards taking control of his lands…and his wife. Calling out to those closest to him, he walked to his tent. Four men stood guard there, one at each corner, and none looked happy.

'Problems, Ansel?' he asked as he approached. All seemed quiet, but their expressions and the very number of them said otherwise. Though this was Ansel's first battle campaign, he trusted the young man to carry out whatever task he so ordered.

'Aye,' Ansel answered in their dialect. 'She is…the lady is… determined.' He shook his head as though he had failed and Brice noticed the beginnings of a bruise on the man's chin.

Brice took hold of the flap of the tent and paused. 'So long as no harm came to her, I do not question your actions.'

Ansel nodded, but there was still a problem that Brice could not identify. Then Stephen approached.

'She nearly escaped three times, Brice,' he explained. 'Once she got as far as the south perimeter of the camp without being seen.' Brice glanced at each of the men guarding the tent, seeing then that several sported new scratches or bruises, and then back at Stephen, who let out a breath and shrugged. 'Blame this on me if you must, but it was the only way to secure her.'

Brice winced at both the words and tone and wondered how they had done it. He nodded to them. 'Bring something for the lady to eat and then seek out your meal. We will proceed once she's eaten.'

The men walked away and Brice lifted the tent flap to one side so he could enter. Bending down to avoid knocking into the top of the tent, he stepped inside and stopped. In spite of only one lantern lighting the darkness, he could see her clearly and his mouth dropped open even as he hardened at the sight before him.

The men had driven big wooden stakes into the ground and tied her to them, wrists and ankles bound together and then to the posts. Her head covering gathered around her neck and a gag sealed her mouth. From her struggles against the bindings, her gown twisted high on her legs, exposing their shapeliness to his gaze. Due to the position of her arms and the shifting of the top of her gown, her breasts thrust against the material, their tightened peaks visible through the soft gown.

Brice swallowed, and then again, his mouth suddenly dry. He stepped farther into the tent and dropped the flap behind him. She began to struggle anew as he approached and her efforts caused her gown to shift more, gifting him with a clear view of her thighs and her hips as she turned and tried to pull away. He found himself clenching and releasing his fists as they ached to slide up the expanse of white, soft skin and cup her bottom. Heat pulsed through him then and he thought of all the places he would caress and kiss before the morn.

She mumbled something against the cloth in her mouth and he realised he could not leave her so. Crouching down beside her, he took out his dagger and slit the side of the gag. 'Easy now, mistress,' he soothed. With a gentle touch, he smoothed her hair from her face and wiped her cheeks.

Tears. She'd been crying. From what little he'd learned of his betrothed, he knew that this sign of weakness would humiliate her and he had little stomach for that now. He went to the small table and poured some wine from the jug into a metal cup and brought it to her.

'Here now, drink this.' He lifted her head and helped her sip until she drank the small amount of wine. After she'd finished, he filled the cup once more and drank it down quickly.

Kneeling at her side, he began to straighten her gown. But when his hand touched her ankle, he could not stop himself from enjoying just a small touch. He slid his hand up to her knee before grasping the hem of the gown. His body urged him to push it higher, to slide up her thigh and between her legs to that place that he could make weep at his caress. Brice fought the desire to explore her body and only her soft words brought him to his senses.

'I pray thee, my lord. Please do not...' she whispered.

She did not move at all, and it was a good thing, for the battle of doing the right thing or following his body's urgings was a near one just then. After a moment that lingered too long, he tugged the length of the gown down to cover her legs and backed away.

The awkwardness between them was broken when Ansel called to him from outside. Brice turned and stepped out, coming back in with a wooden plate for the lady. He placed it on the table and took his dagger once more, sliding it carefully into the knot around her wrists. She gasped as he twisted it, most likely more surprised than anything else, for he took great care not to nick her skin in doing so. It was only when he held out his hand to her that he realised he was still in his hauberk of chainmail and wore his thick leather gloves.

Regardless of the soft look in his gaze at this moment, Gillian did not trust him. Oh, his men had not hurt her yet, but being tied up and gagged and then left for hours on end had tested her patience and courage. Though a virgin, she'd recognised the lust in this man's gaze when he touched her leg and looked at the way her gown had shifted to expose places better left covered. How long she would remain untouched or unused she did not know and dared not ask.

Still, if she was untied, there was a better chance of escape than if she remained trussed like a goose. Gillian accepted his hand and let him pull her up to sit. When she reached for the ropes that bound her legs together and to the other spike, he stopped her.

'Leave them,' he said gruffly, the deep voice and accented words affecting her more than she wished they would. She pulled the edges of her gown as far over her feet as she could and tugged the laces at her neckline tighter, too.

He reached over and dipped a linen square in a bucket by the tent's entrance and then handed it to her to use. Wiping it over her face and neck, she removed the dirt from her struggles and the tears that she'd shed against all of her attempts not to cry. Then, she cleaned her hands and held the cloth out to him. *'Merci,'* she whispered, using one of the few words in his tongue she knew.

He started as she said it, and she realised her error. A poor English maid would not know his French. A poor English woman would know only her English words…or Saxon or Danish ones, but not French. When he replied in his own language, she blinked and shook her head as though she knew none of it. Truly, she could follow most of it when he spoke slowly, but she did not want him or his men to know that. Better to gain what information she could while here and share it with her brother when she got back to Thaxted Keep.

If she returned to her brother.

Gillian shivered then as she realised she might not survive the coming night. After all, these men did not believe her story and thought her a prostitute. If made to…service them…

against her will, she might not even be alive in the morn to try to escape once more. Her body shuddered then, from her head down to her now shoeless feet.

The knight reacted quickly but in an unexpected way, for he called out to the other one, Stephen, and demanded something. Robe? Cloak? Soon, her missing cloak and shoes were handed into the tent. He shook out her cloak and draped it over her shoulders. She grabbed it and pulled it tight around her, taking what protection it could offer her. Soon, after hours spent on the cold ground with little protection from it, her body began to warm under the thick layer of wool. Then, his gentle touch in placing her shoes back on her feet surprised her again. His men had taken them the last time she'd got past them, knowing that she could not go far on the cold ground without them.

When he held the plate in front of her, her stomach growled loudly, giving her no chance to refuse his offer. She took the food—some cooked fowl, a chunk of cheese and another of bread—and ate it. No matter what challenges faced her, she needed to be at her strongest and she continued to tear apart the roasted hen and break apart the cheese and bread until every bit of it was gone. Gillian looked up to find him watching her every move. When he filled a cup for her, she drank it down.

Knowing that this was simply a respite before whatever else he'd planned for her, she knew she should have slowed down and taken her time, but an empty stomach and all the exertions of the day proved her match.

She had barely finished the food and drink when she heard movement outside the tent and the sound of many voices growing closer. Had her brother discovered her missing and followed? Did he now attack to recover her? When the soldier took the plate from her, she gave up all pretence and began to work the ropes around her ankles. Either he ignored her or did not think she could do it, for he left the tent then and she increased her efforts.

If only she had a dagger or her small knife, or something sharp to loosen the knot or cut the ropes! Gillian continued until she heard the words spoken by Stephen to her captor.

'The men are ready.'

Her mind emptied of all thought then and the only thing she could do was struggle against the ropes. Pulling on one, then another, she shook as the thought of what lay ahead pierced her. They would take their pleasure of her now. All of them? Saints in heaven, protect her!

Fighting off the panic that assailed her, Gillian knew she must be in control and seek out a moment when she could escape. To do that, she must be alive. Taking several deep breaths and trying to let out the terror that threatened to control her, she knew what she must do. When the leader entered the tent and approached her, she knew the only way to live through this was through him.

He'd removed his chainmail hauberk and wore only a thick, quilted tunic in its place. His leather gloves were gone, as well. Instead of easing her fears, for she knew that men could tup women in armour or out of it, it increased them for he looked no less the dangerous warrior than before in his battle dress. He crouched near her once more and used his deadly dagger on the ropes until they gave way. Helping her to her feet, he wrapped an arm around her waist when she began to stumble.

'My lord,' she whispered, turning to face him. He did not release her; nay, if truth be told he held her more closely than before. 'I would...see to your needs willingly if you promised not to share me with the others.'

Shocked that she could speak such damning words aloud, she knew she must seem honest in her intentions or all was lost. Gillian reached up and clutched the neckline of his tunic as she promised anything to keep herself alive. 'I wish to warm your bed only, my lord.'

The warrior released her so quickly she nearly fell to the ground. She'd angered him in some way, not pacified him with her promise of pleasure. He grabbed her by the wrist and pulled her to the entrance of the tent.

'Nay, my lord,' she cried out, both in pain from his tight grasp and in fear of being given to the others. 'I beg you not to share me with your men!'

In but a few moments, she stood outside the tent, in front of what seemed to be hundreds of men. Though night-time, the full moon's light alone would have made it possible to see their numbers, but the burning torches spread around the camp made it seem like day. He held her wrist in his iron grasp and pulled her to face him.

'*Oui,* my Lady Gillian, you will warm my bed this night,' he growled through clenched teeth. He knew! He knew who she was! Before she could explain, he tugged her closer until only she could hear his words. 'And I will share my wife with no other man.'

Chapter Three

Gillian searched his face for answers she did not find. He was angry, aye, for it poured off him in waves. She understood now that he'd known her identity the whole while, even as she dissembled and lied. How?

'Who are you?' she asked.

Her brother had told her of the usurper's nobleman on his way to claim their lands as well as herself, but this man who stood before her swore he was not noble. She'd heard his common cursing and seen the way the others called him by name—Brice—and not with the respect due a lord of the realm, even that of the Norman pigs who now infested their lands.

'Brice Fitzwilliam, newly named Lord of Thaxted and baron to his Highness Duke William of Normandy and King of England,' he said loud enough for all his men to hear. 'And your husband,' he said as he offered a slight bow to her.

Their answering cheers shook the night and terrified her. This was the man who would tear her world apart, kill her brother, take her lands and people and conquer her as surely as his bastard duke had ravaged the south of England already.

Fitzwilliam? He was a bastard himself. Now she understood his anger, for her earlier words about noblemen were an insult to his new honour.

'You are not my husband,' she said, refusing to believe that such a thing could be accomplished without her participation or consent.

He laughed then, surprising her and showing a different side to him from what she'd witnessed thus far. His eyes gleamed in merriment and the way his mouth curved into a smile made her body fill with heat. When he turned that smile in her direction, she lost her breath.

'But that can be managed so easily, my lady,' he said, motioning to someone across the clearing. 'At your command.'

An old man, a priest, came forwards from the crowd, followed by a younger man not in priestly garb, but who carried a number of parchments. They stopped in front of her and bowed.

'Lady Gillian,' the older man said respectfully. 'I am Father Henry, late of Taerford.' Turning to the Norman warrior, he spoke softly. 'My lord, Selwyn will read out the marriage contract and disposition of properties and titles.'

So shocked was she by this turn of events, she had not noticed when his tight grasp had loosened or when his hand had clasped hers or when their fingers had entwined. She'd gone from prisoner to betrothed wife in moments and could not comprehend the change. As the young man Selwyn read out the honours and lands bestowed on this Lord Brice Fitzwilliam, who was from Brittany, not Normandy, she tried to think of a way out. A way back to Thaxted Keep; to her brother's protection; to her life as she knew it just months ago.

Instead, she stood with a complete stranger, a foreign knight

raised high by his king, a man who would—if she consented—
control her lands, her people, her person and body as his own.
Gillian knew she must do something, but as she began to pull
from his grasp, he whispered the words to her that would chill
her blood and ensure her co-operation.

'Honoured wife or exiled peasant. Which do you wish to
be this night, Gillian?'

His gaze showed neither gloating nor persuasion when she
met it and she knew he would make certain that her choice
became the reality of her life. Selwyn finished reading out
the contract approved by his king and all eyes watched as she
hesitated.

Something deep inside urged her to be brave and denounce
this enemy, fight off his attempts to take her against her will
and defy her brother's intentions. Surely the priest would not
stand by while she was forced into this marriage or while his
men ravaged her.

Another part of her wanted to stand up and do whatever
she could, put up with what she must in order to protect the
people who lived on their lands against this conqueror. The
noble blood in her veins, though tainted by the circumstances
of her birth, ran back countless generations through her father
and it strengthened her resolve not to stand by while her people
were made to suffer more. If marriage to this warrior would
bring peace to their land, then she would endure it.

'Do you consent to this marriage?' the Breton asked once
more, this time in that voice so tempting that Eve herself would
have fallen again from Paradise to say yes to him.

Though she wished that just once she could be considered only for her own worth and not as some valued com-
modity, Gillian understood the truth of her situation and the

responsibility she bore. Mayhap at another time, she could do something just because she wanted to or could refuse something she objected to, but this was not that time and she had not the luxury of such a choice.

And so, wearing the dirt of the road from her travels and from her attempts to escape, covered in a servant's cloak and standing before hundreds of men she knew not, Gillian surrendered her will and consented to the sham of a marriage. Worse, as she heard that sultry voice of his, pledging himself to her and promising to protect her and honour her, heat poured through every part of her body and sinful images of lying with him filled her thoughts.

When the words were finished and he leaned towards her to seal their agreement with a kiss, she knew exactly how Eve had felt that day when confronted by the devil.

He caught her surprised gasp when he touched his mouth to hers. She stood lost in her thoughts as they said their vows, but he wanted her to understand what she had agreed to. The ease with which she'd bartered herself to him in the tent had filled him with anger, but he tasted her innocence and fear as his lips slid across hers now. Stepping closer, he slipped his arm around her shoulders, both pulling her closer and keeping her from falling.

She did not fight him, but did not participate in the kiss, and Brice felt a small measure of disappointment that the spirit she'd displayed earlier had disappeared now. He wanted to taste her fire and her strength, but all he felt was her fear. Her body trembled in his embrace, so he kissed her lightly and quickly and lifted his head.

Her turquoise eyes stared back at him and he watched as

curiosity, fear and surprise warred within her gaze. She reached up and touched her mouth as though she'd never been kissed. Regardless of her innocence or lack of participation, his body responded to the taste of her soft lips and to the promise of holding her close to him in his bed. He would slide his hands beneath her gown and caress every part of her before the sun's light touched the camp once more.

Whether she understood it or not, her body did, for she shuddered as Brice stared into her eyes, wanting her naked and writhing at his every caress. She would warm his bed this night and every other one from this time forwards and he would show her such pleasure that she would never regret giving her consent. He tore his gaze from hers and examined her from the top of her head to her feet.

Her lush hips promised healthy babes and once he removed her brother from their lands and secured this area for William, he intended to breed many with her. All of them would bear his name, unlike his own father, for Brice had married the woman who would give him children. Now that she was in his possession, everything he'd ever wanted, everything he'd laboured for and worked for was within his reach.

Taking her hand and turning her towards his men, he held their joined hands up and claimed her.

'Lady Gillian of Thaxted,' he called out loudly. 'My wife!' The cheering began slowly and spread out through the camp as one and all acknowledged his marriage and saluted his wife. He nodded to Stephen, who stepped forwards and bowed to Gillian. 'Take the lady to my tent and guard her until I arrive,' he ordered.

Brice had no doubt that the words spoken by her or promises made would fade as soon as she realised what she'd done.

Therefore only consummation would make her understand she was now his and prevent any claim that could nullify their vows. Until that was accomplished and their marriage was acknowledged by all parties, he would protect her as the treasure she was.

Stephen approached and he felt her body tense. His man bowed to her and held out his arm to escort her as befit a lady and his wife. 'My lady?'

Brice held his breath as he waited for her to bolt, but she placed her hand on Stephen's arm and walked at his side towards his tent. Brice had to see to many tasks before he could retire for the night and if he appeared to hurry none of his men mentioned it.

An hour or two later, after messages had been sent and more guards set to watch around their camp, he stood in front of his tent and wondered which woman—the honoured wife or the escaping peasant—he would find within. Reaching out, he lifted the flap and entered.

Though she heard his approach and entrance into the tent, Gillian did not rise or look up to meet his gaze. As yet uncertain of the situation and the man involved, she'd pondered her options for the last hour or two. And that was after spending a while in complete shock over her new circumstances. Instead of becoming used to the ever-present changes in her life, she was truly tired of it.

Her plan to escape her half-brother's control and to avoid this marriage and seek refuge in the convent had failed. Oh, it was ill advised at best from the beginning, but it was a better plan than the first three times she'd tried it. Both her brother's threats of repeating the punishments he'd already applied for any future attempts and her need to flee his machinations had brought her to this.

She dared not seek Oremund's help now. She could not make it to the convent. She had not... Sighing, Gillian knew she was out of choices.

'Lady?' His deep voice broke into her reverie and forced her gaze up to his.

How had she ever mistaken him for anything other than the leader he was? Even if she discounted his lack of a banner proclaiming his insignia, even if she ignored the uncouth and foul language she'd heard him use, even believing Oremund's stories about the Norman—nay, Breton—and his plans, there was no way to ignore the inherent nobility of the man standing before her now.

He'd removed his chainmail and other accoutrements of fighting and war and stood there as just a man. Yet now he seemed even more dangerous than before.

He was tall, tall enough that he had to crouch down to walk farther into the tent and not hit the top of it with his head. He was large, with broad shoulders that bespoke years of training in his craft. He was...waiting. She swallowed deeply then as she realised he watched her perusal of him and allowed it. Gillian lowered her gaze to her clasped hands and waited quietly.

'Did they bring you fresh water and see to your comforts?' he asked softly. Without even lifting her head, she could see him moving closer to her. 'Do you need something to drink or eat?'

With the time before he consummated their marriage running out, she decided to try one last time to dissuade him from his purpose.

'My lord,' she said quietly as she rose to her feet and stood before him, 'I need nothing from you save your grant of safe passage to the convent.'

The tension between and around them grew as she waited on his word. When silence was her only answer, she lifted her head and looked at him. His brown eyes darkened even more as the intensity and heat of his gaze moved over her.

'You have asked for one of the two things I could not grant you, lady, even if I wished it to be so.'

Had he done it a-purpose? He'd phrased his words so that she had to ask about the other. Did he know of her unseemly curiosity, something her brother and their father had decried as a flaw in her character? Her heart began to pound in her chest as he reached out and took her hand in his, tugging her even closer. Try as she might, Gillian could not stop the words from spilling out.

'What is the other?' She held her breath as he lifted her hand to his mouth and kissed the inside of her wrist. He allowed his lips to rest there for a moment longer than necessary before looking back at her.

'I could not let you greet the morning as a maiden still,' he said.

Shaking her head, she pulled her hand from his grasp. Or tried to, for his fingers held tight and did not allow her to free herself. 'My lord…'

'My lady,' he replied.

'I beg you…' Her voice caught as he slid the sleeve of her gown down her arm and followed it with his mouth, placing heated kiss after heated kiss along the exposed skin there.

Flames seemed to grow within her and she could not find the thoughts and arguments that seemed so coherent just moments before. Her body trembled at his intimate touch and she reached her free hand up to pry loose his hold.

'Nay, my lady,' he whispered against her skin, not even pausing in his attentions as he caught her hand and placed it on his chest. 'I could not allow it.'

With her hands held so, she was forced to lean closer to him. She searched his face for any sign that he would relent, but there was none. And when he turned to look at her and she recognised the glint of desire in his eyes, she knew she had no chance of escaping his intentions. Even when he released her hands, it was only for a moment and only to untie her veil and remove it. He tossed the linen aside and took her into his embrace, drawing her even nearer. When his mouth descended and touched hers, she lost her wits completely and every attempt to focus on her plan, a plan, any plan, failed as her body fell under his spell.

This kiss began much as his first had, but then it changed quickly into something seeking, something demanding, something seducing. She lost her breath as he turned his face and took control of her mouth and her body. Gillian felt his hands slide up onto her shoulders and then into her hair as she gave herself over to the kiss. Opening to him as his tongue touched her lips, she allowed him his way and felt the shivers pulse through her body. The thought that she'd never been kissed in such a bold and possessive manner flitted through her mind for a moment.

When he relinquished his hold of her hair and slid one hand slowly down her body, touching and caressing her neck and then her breasts and stopping to rest splayed over her belly, she pulled away from his kiss and tried to breathe. A kiss was one thing, but to touch her in such an intimate way was…

Decadent.

Forbidden.

Scandalous.

He did not force her to accept his touch, but he did not remove his hand from its place too close to the junction of her thighs. A place she'd not truly thought much about before, but that now ached for something unknown. And that ache spread as she saw the desire burning in his gaze as he waited on her.

'This is ill advised, my lord,' she forced out. 'We know nothing of each other and yet you would bed me here, now?'

His hand remained in place, making it impossible to cool the heat that poured through her. But she must, if she was to avoid this next step.

'The king has granted me these lands, this title and you, lady. In spite of your efforts and those of your brother—' he began quietly.

'Half,' she interrupted. His brows gathered in a frown. 'My half-brother,' she explained.

'Half or full matters not to me or the king,' he said and then he shook his head. 'In spite of the efforts to keep me from said lands and wife, I have found you and I will not risk any more delays or disappearances. I need to know nothing more than that you are my legally wedded…' before she could think of another tack to take, he leaned down and kissed her again and continued '…and soon-to-be-bedded wife.'

Something finally sparked inside her, whether foolishness or bravery she knew not, and she pulled away once more.

'And if you lay dead after the coming battle, I will know

nothing of you save your name. Does that not worry you?'
From the entirely confident look on his face, she knew what
his answer would be.

'I will not lose the coming battle, lady. If anyone is dead
after it, it will be your brother.'

His words startled her, for she'd not truly thought about
the whole process enough. Oh, aye, she knew there would
be a fight to gain control of Thaxted and she knew some
would be injured or perish. God forgive her, she even knew
of several names she hoped would be on one or the other of
those lists, but so would others—others innocent of this game
played between kings and nobles. Always the innocents paid
the price.

'Forgive me for those words, Gillian,' he said, taking her
by her shoulders. 'War is not easy for any of those who fight
and I ask your pardon for taunting you with words of your
brother's death.'

He'd shocked her again, he knew, for her turquoise eyes grew
wide and her mouth dropped open. He was not a fool when it
came to seducing women and yet all of his skills seemed to
have deserted him when he needed them most. He must claim
her this night. He must make her his wife in truth so that, no
matter what happened in the coming battles, she would have
the protection of his friends and even the king. Brice began
once more to seduce her into his bed.

'We will have many days to come to know each other better,
Gillian. Let us take this first step now,' he whispered, lifting
the long curls off her shoulders and smoothing them down her
back.

She shivered under his touch, whether she knew it or not, as
her body readied itself for him. Brice leaned down and kissed

her, not waiting for any questions or protests. At first she remained still, but when he probed gently with his tongue and began to tease and touch hers, Gillian closed her eyes and accepted the intimate invasion once more. He plied her with one kiss after another until he could hear her breathing deeply. But it was the breathy sigh that nearly made him lose control.

Although he was the one thinking his way through this encounter, his body reacted to the sounds of her innocent excitement and each sigh sent more blood rushing to his groin, hardening him until he felt as though he would explode.

Sliding one arm behind her shoulders and then scooping her up into his embrace, Brice kissed her again as he carried her to his pallet and knelt down to place her on its surface. Although clean, he knew it lacked the level of comfort and luxury she was used to having. The thought that he was taking her on a thin pallet in a tent in the middle of an armed camp struck him as he eased his arm out from beneath her legs.

A lady deserved better than to be tupped like a camp follower. A lady should be wooed and willing to give up her virginity. A lady wife should be honoured and taken gently in comfort and privacy.

Allowing only a moment of regret at the circumstances and surroundings, Brice guided Gillian down onto the pallet and stretched out at her side, his arm still holding her around her shoulders. When he was forced to relinquish her mouth, he kissed the soft skin along her jaw and her ear. Pleased when her body trembled in his embrace, he traced the outline of her lips with a finger. Brice followed the contours of her jaw, down to her neck and then across the swell of her breasts until he reached the laces on her gown. She gasped when he tugged them loose and then grabbed his hand to halt his progress.

'Someone might come in,' she whispered.

Though he knew no one would dare interrupt him, he tried to soothe her fear. 'Unless this tent is on fire, no one will enter.'

Brice leaned down once more and kissed the skin on her neck, easing the ties loose as he did so. His fingers grazed the swells of her breasts as he slipped them inside the gown. Gillian arched into his hand when he touched the tips of her breasts, sucking in a breath as he continued to caress there. He felt himself surge then, ready to finish the act in spite of his efforts to follow a leisurely path and ensure the lady's— his wife's—pleasure.

He glanced at her face and saw that she lay with her eyes closed tightly. Only her mouth gave any sign that his attempts to ease her way were working. As he watched, she worried her lower lip with the edges of her teeth and then licked them with her tongue. Every movement and sound she made sent chills through his body and caused the blood in his veins to thunder through him. Though he wanted to tear off her garments and claim her, he settled for something more subtle.

Still watching her face, he slid his hand down, using the back of it to touch her breasts, stomach and then her thighs. She squirmed in his arms, her innocent body responding to his caresses even though she most likely understood it not. Then, when his hand slid over the tops of her legs and touched the place he craved to see, she gasped loudly and tried to sit up.

'Nay, sweetling,' he whispered, placing his hand over her and holding her still. 'Let me show you the pleasure that can be between man and woman,' he said, moving his hand ever so slightly and meeting her gaze as he did. 'Between a husband and wife,' he continued as he paused to gather the length of her gown in his hand. Her skin, as he touched it, was soft and smooth and her legs, exposed now to his gaze, were shapely and long. He almost had the gown out of his way when she grabbed his wrist.

'They can hear us, my lord. They can hear every sound we make.'

This was one of the reasons he never took virgins to his bed or sought them out—their shyness interfered with the level of pleasure they could reach. And a bastard such as he was never good enough to have access to a virgin, especially a well- or high-born one like his wife was.

'I assure you they have orders not to disturb our privacy, lady. Any sounds you or I make will be ignored, if heard at all over the din of the camp. Worry not on this.'

Brice placed his hand on the bare skin of her thigh and began to reach to touch the curls still hidden by her gown when she started again. This time she managed to push back out of his embrace.

'Did you hear that?' she whispered. 'Someone is just outside the tent.' Her eyes flitted from one side of the tent to the other and then to the entrance.

He listened, but heard nothing. If it would ease her in this, Brice decided he would make certain his orders were being followed. He doubted any of his men would have come close to his tent, but he nodded to her and stood up, tugging his braes so that they covered the proof of his arousal. Stepping to the flap of the tent, he lifted it and looked outside.

The guards stood in their positions some distance away. He could detect no movements or sounds adjacent to the tent or in the immediate area. As he turned back to tell her, he hoped that this would give her the reassurance she needed to yield to him.

He never saw the weapon hurtling at him from the shadows of the tent until it struck. Then it was too late.

Chapter Four

Gillian grabbed his tunic as he fell, making certain he landed inside the tent. Unable to believe her luck, she threw the heavy sword in its scabbard into the corner and looked for her cloak. She stepped over the unconscious knight and prepared to escape once more. Then she realised he'd not moved since landing face down on the ground there.

Had she killed him? That was never her intent, but she had swung the hilt of the sword as hard as she could at his head to stop him. Crouching down next to him, she lifted his shoulder up and slid her hand down near his mouth and nose. The heat of his breath touched her skin and she sighed in relief. Murder was never her intent.

She released his shoulder and let him lie as he fell, for there was not time and she had not the strength to move or secure him. Gillian did reach down and take the dagger from its sheath inside the cross-garters on his leg where she'd watched him place it. At least it would give her some protection as she made her escape. Peeking out of the tent, she saw that his men, as he'd said, stood some distance away.

Good. If the rest of his words about not paying attention to the goings-on in their leader's tent were true, she could sneak away and get to the convent, less than a mile or so from here. Kneeling down, she crept on hands and knees away from the tent until she reached the edge of the forest, and then she ran. At the river she turned and ran along it, knowing that it flowed next to the convent's walls.

Gillian never looked back, never paused, and never slowed as she followed the water to her goal. When she broke through the last copse of trees between her and safety, she skidded to a stop, unable to breathe and unable to believe her eyes. A line of knights, all of them mounted, sat between her and the convent walls.

Her eyes burned with tears of frustration as she realised that she would never outrun these men. Bending over, she drew in deep breaths, trying to calm her racing pulse and the fear that now filled her. If these men were here, their leader would have known where she would flee. He had known all along!

The men said nothing, only waiting as though it was their custom to chase down their lord's wife in the middle of the night. When she could breathe evenly again, she stood and adjusted her cloak and veil and prepared to be dragged or escorted back to the camp…and to her husband. She shivered then, knowing that he would probably react as her brother had when she'd thwarted his plans—with anger and punishment. The Breton had new ways to punish her wilfulness and her assault on him, and she feared the coming night more now than she had before.

The sound of something breaking through the undergrowth behind and the way the men turned to look made her skin turn to gooseflesh. Gillian slid the dagger into her palm and pivoted towards the trees. It was not the size of the horse that terrified her, nor the length of the sword brandished in her direction. Nay, not those things, but the hardened expression of pure rage that filled the Breton warrior's face as he beheld her standing there.

He'd not taken time to don his mail or even his helm, and indeed she could see blood streaming down the side of his face along the line of his hair and down his neck from the wound on his head. She swallowed deeply and offered up a quick plea for the forgiveness of her sins to the Almighty, for Gillian did not doubt that her death was imminent. It took every bit of courage and strength she had not to back away when he leapt down from the horse and approached her in slow, measured steps. She wiped her shaking, sweaty palms against her cloak and waited to meet her fate.

He stopped a few paces from her and seemed to realise then that he still threatened her with the sword in his hand. Without taking his eyes from hers, he slid the deadly steel blade back into its scabbard. She startled at his first step nearer.

'Give me the dagger,' he whispered harshly, holding his hand out to her.

She'd forgotten she held it, still frightened by the rage in his eyes, and, for a moment, she thought of the possibility of using it against him. But what would it gain her other than a swift death and the damnation of her eternal soul? Even now gazing into his angry face, Gillian knew that his death would help nothing…and it was not something she wished for even at her weakest moments.

Letting out the breath she'd held in for all those moments, Gillian turned the dagger and handed it, hilt first, to the Breton. So quickly that she nearly missed it, a flash of relief brightened the stark, masculine angles of his face, softening it for one fleeting moment. Then, the anger was back as he slipped the dagger back from where she'd stolen it.

Borrowed it.

One of the warriors called out something from behind her and she tried to translate his words, but he spoke too quickly. The Breton answered him in the same tongue, but whether he did it a-purpose or because of fear clouding her mind, she did not understand him, either. Finally, after an exchange of words that lasted several minutes, he looked back at her and shook his head.

Gillian searched her thoughts for something to say. Something that could explain or at least mitigate what she'd done to him. But, truly, how did one explain away knocking another person out? She knew what she'd done; he knew it, as well. All that was left was for him to apply whatever punishment he'd decided upon. Since she knew he wanted her alive, Gillian prepared herself. She'd already survived beatings and whippings by her half-brother, so she believed she could survive whatever this man would deal out to her.

So when, with a nod at his men behind her, he mounted his horse, ordered them to bring her with them and then rode off towards his camp, she could do nothing but stare. That was until a horse's nose butted her on the shoulder from behind and she stumbled.

'Go, lady,' the knight on the horse ordered.

At first, she did not understand and she looked around to see the knights still on their horses, some closer to her, some still nearer to the convent walls.

'Go,' he said, nodding at the forest, 'follow the same path back to camp.'

It was not that she could not understand his words then, she just could not comprehend his orders. She was to walk back to the camp? Alone? Where had their leader gone?

'Lord Brice said to walk back to the camp and think on your sins as you do so,' the one named Stephen said. The other men laughed then, apparently knowing more about her sins than she'd have liked. 'He awaits you there.'

Her stomach gripped then as she realised that this was not his punishment, this was but the prelude to whatever he planned. And she must walk back to face it. She shook her head until the knight called out to her once more.

'Now, lady,' he said. 'Or he ordered me to tie you to my horse and drag you back.' His voice lowered then and Gillian thought she recognised a touch of regret in his tone. 'It is not that far and I am certain you would rather arrive there on your feet and not trussed up like some slave.'

He was offering her dignity. Outmanned and outmanoeuvred, certainly for the moment, Gillian decided to acquiesce. She nodded at him and began walking. It would give her time to think of another plan.

The cold air quickly seeped through her cloak as she traced her path back to the river's edge and then along it. Four knights, two before and two behind, escorted her. Though their pace was slow for men on horseback, it was fast enough that she struggled after only a few minutes. Most likely, two days of walking and the events of the night so far were the cause of her growing exhaustion. And the recent run from the camp here added to the pain in her legs and the weariness that spread through her.

Tugging her cloak closer and pulling the hood of it forwards to cover her head, she focused her thoughts on placing one foot in front of the other. After some time, more than Gillian remembered it taking to cover the distance, they reached the turn in the path that took them towards the road, and a while later the camp. More than once, a horse nudged her along. More than once, she waved them off to stop and catch her breath. And more than once, she wished she could think of a way to evade them and their lord.

But all she could do was walk and think.

And worry.

Oh, not over any sins she might have committed as their lord had ordered, but about the rest of the coming night. And the coming day which would see his forces pitted against her half-brother and his allies. When the fires of the camp came into view, Gillian found that most everything disappeared from her list of things to worry over, except the one about the coming night. The knights led her back to his tent, which was now surrounded by guards, and called out to their lord. At his word, Stephen motioned her forwards.

After a deep breath, Gillian walked up to the tent and lifted the flap to enter.

Brice sat waiting for her arrival and pondered all the mistakes he'd made in dealing with Lady Gillian of Thaxted. Once his anger cooled, even he could see the resemblance to the wedding-night farce experienced by his friend Giles, now Lord of Taerford. And that did not please him at all, for it only served to remind him of his own boast that he would not have those kinds of problems when he claimed his bride.

Now, with his head still pounding from being hit with his own sword and with his runaway bride standing outside his tent, he hoped word of this debacle would not reach Giles or his lady Fayth for some time. And hopefully he could recover from the disastrous start and get his marriage, and the invasion of his keep, underway in a more successful manner. Taking a mouthful of the ale from his cup, he touched the egg-sized lump on his head to see if it had stopped bleeding yet. Bringing away nothing on his fingers, he drank again, hoping the ale would ease the anger and the pain.

He heard Stephen's call from outside and waited for her to enter. Brice had chosen to get away from her when his fury about her attack and her disobedience nearly overwhelmed his better judgement, for he was not a man to take his anger out on others and he did not wish to do so now. Well, he might wish to do it, but he would not.

Gillian stepped into the tent, and it suddenly felt much smaller than it had. He watched as she moved a few paces in and let the flap drop back into place. From the corner where he sat on a stool he waited for her to see him. Her reaction, when she did, was not a good one, for she gasped and backed up towards the entrance. He looked in the direction of her gaze and realised that the bloodied rags he'd used in cleaning the gash on his head lay on the ground at his feet.

'I...I...' she began to stutter.

'Do not make some false claim of regret, lady,' he warned, kicking the rags out of his way and standing before her. 'You wanted to escape, I was in your way, and you removed me.' He crossed his arms over his chest and allowed himself a moment of enjoyment at her discomfort. He knew, though, that the way she reacted to his accusation was important in coming to know her better.

Gillian let out a loud sigh and pushed her loosened hair back out of her face. Her bedraggled appearance in no way marred her beauty; instead, it made him want to wrap her in his arms and kiss away the worries that caused the crease to deepen between her brows.

'You are correct, my lord,' she said softly. 'My only intention was to escape. You were in my way.'

'Why?' he asked. The word surprised him until he realised that he did want to know her reasons for running from him. 'Did you run from me in particular? From this marriage?' She looked as though she sought a way out of answering, so he asked again. 'You spoke the vows in front of the priest and witnesses. You pledged yourself to me. So, lady, why did you run?'

'I ran from you. I ran from this marriage. I just ran,' she said in a voice so low he nearly missed it. She looked away from him, too, not meeting his gaze, but staring down at her hands while she spoke. Hands that twisted the cloth of her cloak in a tight spiral.

He suspected that she knew he would intercept any of her attempts to get to the convent, but why had she not run back to her brother's protection?

'Why the convent?' He took a step towards her, but paused when she backed away. Likely she feared his anger even now.

'I would be welcome there. The reverend mother said I would be welcomed into their community.'

'And your brother would not welcome your return to him?' he asked.

The stricken expression at his words told him more than he ever expected to learn, for her face paled and her eyes filled with pain and fear. Brice reached out for her, but she moved farther away from him. Filled with uncertainty about how to proceed with her, he could tell by watching the lady that exhaustion threatened to overwhelm her even now.

It had been his plan—having her walk back to the camp would tire her out and make another attempt to escape this night nearly impossible. Now, as he watched her struggle to remain standing even while trying to appear strong, he understood the strength of her pride and her determination.

She was a worthy opponent, but would be a better lady to their people and a wife to him—if he could gain her trust and co-operation. Swiving her in this tent now would not accomplish that. Not consummating the marriage was not a choice, for if she did reach the convent it would cause a complicated mess that would take months or years to sort through. And he knew to the marrow of his bones that she would try again. Still, he shook his head and surrendered to the inevitable.

'Seek your rest, lady,' he said, pointing to the pallet.

She started and glanced between him and the pile of blankets they'd occupied not long ago. 'I do not understand.'

'It is nearly the middle of the night,' he began. 'Many new challenges face us in the morn, so seek your rest.'

Brice turned away and began to pick up the rags from the ground. She remained still where she stood, not yet moving to the pallet. So, he went over, lifted up several of the blankets and motioned for her to lie down. As though prepared for him to attack her at any moment, Lady Gillian crept to the pallet and sat down without ever taking her gaze from him. She started to untie her cloak, but then wrapped its length around her and lay down.

Brice layered several blankets over her and tried not to think about her presence in his tent. He tried not to think about the lovely, feminine body under those blankets. He especially tried not to remember the way she sounded, the way she gasped so softly as he slid his hand nearer to her womanly flesh. But when she loosened her veil and her hair spread around her head, he hardened in immediate response to her innocent actions and he nearly lost that battle.

Realising that his body had readied for taking her and distraction was necessary, he walked over to finish his tasks. He should call Ernaut to see to cleaning and arranging things, but that could wait until morning. After securing his sword where she could not reach it easily, he gathered the soiled rags and tossed them out of the tent flap. He busied himself with other menial tasks, all to keep himself from tearing off the blankets, freeing her from her cloak and garments and ploughing her as deeply and fervently as he wanted to do.

A short while later, the sound of clattering teeth filled the small space. Brice turned and walked closer to her. Now he could see that her whole body shivered beneath her cloak and the blankets. His own breath floated in front of him in the cold night's air, making him realise that she must be chilled to the bone from both her run to escape, her walk back to the camp and the absence of any fire or hearth to warm her in the tent.

It was exactly the discomfort he'd wanted her to feel when he gave the orders, but now, watching it, he found he did not like the results. He secured the flap of the tent and after removing his dagger and slipping it under the edge of the pallet, he lifted the blankets and slid in behind the lady.

Since she lay on her side facing away from him, he shifted closer until her back touched his chest and wrapped his arms around her to hold her close. She reacted immediately, her body rigid as she ceased all movements. So still did she lie that he could not even feel her taking breath into her lungs.

'Be at ease, lady,' he whispered to her. 'I seek but to warm you so that your teeth stop making those infernal noises when they clatter from the cold and I can get some rest.'

Gathering the folds of her cloak in his hand, he tucked them tightly around her and moved one leg against hers to give her some warmth. Brice waited on her protests, but none came. After a few minutes, her teeth did indeed stop their clattering. It was another little while before her shivering stopped.

'Though I meant for you to suffer after what you did, I did not intend for the punishment to be so severe,' he whispered as he felt her body relax against his.

He expected no reply, for his words were as close to an explanation as he would go, as close to an apology as he would permit himself to offer. But, as she had in most things since he'd first heard of Lady Gillian of Thaxted, she surprised him once more.

'And though I meant to knock you out of your senses, I did not mean to wound you so deeply,' she whispered back.

Brice could not stop his laughter then, releasing her for a moment and falling on to his back as he did. Then, he rolled against her once more, gathering her into his arms and settling back into their comfortable position.

'Just so, lady. I suspect we may be well suited for each other after all.'

He listened for another reply, but none came, and soon he was met only by the deep, even breaths that spoke of sleep. Now that her shivering had ceased and the warmth of their bodies together increased, Brice could feel the pull of sleep lulling him to it. He might as well get a few hours of rest, before taking the next step with his new wife.

Oh, he knew she thought herself safe from his attentions, but his delay would only last until morning. Though she might have fallen asleep a virgin this night, he planned that she would not be one by the next. Or by the time they rose to face the challenges on the morrow.

Chapter Five

After the dampness of the evening had allowed the cold to seep into the very marrow of her bones, Gillian enjoyed the heat that pulsed through her. As she shifted around within the tight cocoon formed by her cloak and the blankets on the pallet, she realised she was also encircled by the source of the heat. As the sounds of a camp stirring to life began around her, she opened her eyes to find him, her husband, draped over her.

And staring right back at her.

It took but a moment for her to comprehend his intent before he leaned even closer and touched his lips to hers. With the blankets and her cloak and his arms holding her so tight, she could not move away. Or so she told herself that was the reason, but once his mouth took hers, she could think of nothing else but him.

He held her cradled with one arm under her back as he moved the other across her stomach to rest on her hip. The same feelings, the same heat that had rippled through her the last time he touched her like this did so again and her body shivered under his hands.

'Are you cold?' he asked softly, lifting back from the kiss just enough to see her face.

'Nay.' Gillian shook her head though another shudder shook her body even as she spoke. 'I think not,' she admitted. Then as his gentle, exploring touch ignited a path of fire across her stomach and down towards her legs, she said again, 'Nay.'

He smiled then and her heart seemed to beat faster. He moved his hand along her hip and down her leg, and breathing became difficult as her lungs gasped and strained for even breath. But when he gathered the edge of her gown and tunic in his large hand and began to slide it up her legs, her body became a thing she could not recognise.

The skin of her thighs shivered beneath her gown as his hand glided over her and the blood and heat rushed through her veins to pool between her legs. For the ten-and-nine years of her life, she'd rarely had cause to take notice of the sensitive nature of that area, but now, with his attentions last night and this morn, it ached in a way that seemed almost pleasurable.

Without waiting for her permission and certainly not waiting for her to object, he held her closer and kissed her again—this time until she lost her breath and he felt her body press against his. He chuckled against her mouth, continuing to touch and taste her with his tongue even as he stroked closer and closer to that intimate place.

She knew his intent. She knew he would join with her and make her his wife in reality, but all the arguments she'd convinced herself of evaporated in the heat of his onslaught. Having sampled it last night before she tried to escape, she wondered now if fear of this unknown but provocative man and the feelings he made her body experience were what had driven her to run. When his fingers slipped between her legs, Gillian's body arched and tightened, renewing and escalating those feelings and that same fear and need to escape.

Drawing back, she tried to move away from his touch, but the blankets and his arm held her to him. In spite of her movements, he never stopped his advance, his fingers dipping and stroking against the sensitive folds there, making her centre tighten and throb. She lifted her mouth from his and took in a breath, preparing to argue or fight her way out, when his expression stopped her.

She knew in her heart that this was simply a man, a new nobleman, claiming what and whom he considered his. It was about marking her in a way that would touch her body, heart and soul, and in a way that she would never be able to forget or ignore. But when she looked in his eyes and saw the wanting and the desire there, Gillian was prepared to believe it was about a man wanting a woman…a man wanting her.

And in a way that no man had ever wanted her before.

Even as her doubts clamoured in her mind to stop her, she allowed herself to believe it, for it had been too many years of not being wanted by anyone, and the pain and loneliness of such a state screamed out to be banished from her soul.

Gillian closed her eyes and allowed his kiss and his touch, even knowing what would happen. Even knowing that she could never turn back if she let him join with her.

Brice felt the moment she gave up her fight for her mouth and her body softened next to him. He did not know her reasons, for last night's attempts had ended with him unconscious and bleeding, but his body, hardened and ready, urged him past any hesitation to claim her as his own.

As his wife.

Moments before, his actions had been to coax and seduce her, now he touched and kissed to pleasure her. Though he wished that the first time joining with her could be in a more comfortable place and with the privacy of a secure bedchamber, Brice knew that the rest of his plans were based on having his marriage able to withstand any challenge of church or king and that meant he would not wait. The sounds of the camp waking to daylight and preparing for battle meant he could not.

He teased her mouth, nipping at her lips and then kissing her deeply, touching his tongue to hers and suckling on hers as he would soon do to her breasts and even that place where his fingers stroked now. She did not open her eyes, but her body responded to his attentions—and his to hers. His member grew longer and harder and lay between their bodies, waiting.

Brice moved his hand and used his fingers to open her and stroked deeper and harder, enjoying the heat and wetness that poured from her body. She gasped, and then again as he slid his leg between hers.

'Open for me, lady,' he whispered, smiling as she let her legs relax. 'Let me pleasure you, wife.' He who had never had hopes of a wife such as her, who had never had dreams of titles or lands, now held them all in his arms.

Somehow she'd managed to free herself from the layers of clothing and woollen blankets and she grasped his hand. 'Your men...' she whispered. 'They will hear us.'

Though her hand encircled his wrist, he did not stop his movements, rubbing against the slippery folds and then even sliding one finger deep inside her. A moan escaped her now and she stared into his eyes, waiting.

'It matters not to me. For if they hear or not, lady, you will be mine,' he promised.

He stopped his caresses and met her gaze, waiting for her reaction and to see if she would allow him to go on—at least without a fight, for he'd prepared himself for taking her virtue now, seduction and pleasure being his preferred method.

Though he never expected it, it was her body that answered, arching against his hand, demanding more of the pleasure he'd begun. No fool, he watched her intently to see if she agreed. Her turquoise eyes darkened in that moment and she closed them as she kissed him. It was an innocent one, only a touch of her lips to his, but he accepted it as her consent and touched her once more.

Finding the hardened nub hidden deep in the folds, he touched it, spreading the wetness of her arousal and caressing it in long, slow strokes. She gasped against his mouth with each touch, so he slid two fingers inside, moving deeply within her and enjoying her reactions as she now urged his hand on with her grasp.

Knowing she was ready, he removed his hand for a moment and loosened the ties of his braes, freeing himself. She mumbled some words at him, so as soon as he was ready he touched her again. Placing himself between her legs, he replaced his hand with his erection and stroked it along the cleft, watching now from above as she met his gaze and was unable to hide her body's excitement from him.

Her mouth lay open slightly, and her chest rose and fell quickly as she breathed in shallow gasps. Brice wished he had more time, wanted to have more time to see to her complete pleasure, but the demands of the day moved forwards, his men grew closer to the tent and he could delay no longer. Positioning his body, he guided his erection between her legs and pressed it into the tightness there.

His body reacted as if he were a young, untried boy, and the feel of the grip of her core around him drew him in further and faster than he'd meant to go. As he settled into her body, he whispered to her. 'Wife.' Withdrawing and filling her again, he moaned, 'Mine now.'

All the melting, all the trembling and shivering she'd been feeling fled as he entered her. In that moment, her body stopped its progress along the path of pleasure he'd created and she felt only pressure and a stretching burn as he filled her with that part of him that stood ready.

He thrust once, twice and a third time and then stopped. His expression changed quickly from the desire and passion that had tempted her to fall, to one of struggle and then a blankness she could not read. He breathed harshly over her, turning his face away and not meeting her eyes. Though his arms supported most of his weight, they shook in exertion and she waited for what was to come next.

She waited for the pleasure to overtake her. She waited to make the noises that she'd overheard from other couples while they...did this. She waited to lose control and be overwhelmed by temptation and the sin of lust.

She still waited.

He eased his body from hers and then struggled against the blankets and cloak to free himself. Gillian simply watched, a strange detachment filling her as though she peered through another's eyes at the scene. If she were being truthful with herself, she wanted to cry for something lost, for something that did not happen, for...something she could not identify.

Once he'd loosened the blankets, she tugged her cloak from under her and pulled the edge of her gown and tunic down over her bare legs. Gillian could not make herself look at him as he stood and walked away from the pallet. She took advantage of the moment to scramble to her feet and stand, too.

Tugging on the laces of her cloak, she released it and was able to untie the length of veil that lay tight around her neck. Gathering her hair in her hand, she combed through it with her fingers, trying to ease out the tangles from its length.

And still she wanted to cry.

It was all the more distressing because Gillian never cried. Ranted, screamed, argued or cursed, God forgive her, on some particularly aggravating occasions, but never did she cry. Yet as she stood in the middle of his tent, watching him out of the corner of her eye, the tightness in her throat grew stronger and the burning in her eyes threatened to release torrents. It could only be worse if he attempted to be kind now.

'Lady,' he said softly as he approached, holding out a cup to her, 'This is a soldier's tent, not set up for the comforts of a woman. I...' He stumbled over whatever words he wanted to say, but she interrupted him, instead.

'I require a few moments of privacy, my lord,' she said in as demanding a voice as she could muster. The strange pain swirled inside her heart and soul as she struggled to keep the tears under control. 'And I need to relieve myself.'

Her brother always withered when confronted with her bold-ness and so this man seemed to also, for after handing her the cup filled with ale, he left the tent for a few moments. When he returned he carried a jug, a small bowl and some cloths.

'If you would like to wash first, I will escort you to a place...'

Without meeting his gaze, she watched the red blush creep up into his cheeks, surprised that a man such as this could be squeamish about the privy details of a woman. She reached out and took the jug and bowl from him and put them on the small table near the pallet. When she turned back to thank him, she saw only his back as he left the tent.

She fought off the tears as she poured the hot water into the bowl and prepared to wash. She fought them off as she cleaned away the signs of her lost virtue. But when she finished her ablutions and gazed around the stark tent where such a life-changing yet somehow disappointing event had occurred, the tears won and she fought them no more. Sinking to her knees, Gillian allowed them to flow, hoping it would gain her some relief from the pain and disillusionment that filled her now. Some minutes later, she heard Brice's deep voice from outside the tent.

'Lady Gillian?' he asked. 'I will escort you now, if you are ready.'

Sighing, she used the last clean cloth to wash her face. Gathering her hair into a rough braid, she tucked it inside the veil and placed it back over her head. Releasing another deep breath, Gillian moved to the entrance and lifted the flap aside as she placed her cloak around her shoulders.

The cold air surrounded her as she stepped out into the bright daylight. Though she thought those nearby had stopped and stared the moment she left the tent, they all quickly returned to their tasks. She spotted the pile of bloodied rags on the ground and dropped the one she carried balled up in her fist with them, hoping no one would notice her do it. Taking a few steps more, she spied Brice with a small group of his men, conversing quietly as she approached.

'Good morrow, my lady,' a young man called out to her. Not raising her head enough for them to see that she'd been crying, she nodded at the man. Bowing slightly to her, he smiled.

'I will have food ready for you to break your fast when you return.'

'My thanks for your kindness, sir,' she said softly, hoping that Brice would escort her away soon.

'No "sir", this one, lady,' he said, cuffing the young man on the ear. 'This is my worthless squire, Ernaut. He will see to your needs until we can secure a maid to serve you.'

'My pleasure, Lady Gillian.' She peeked to see if he mocked her with his words, but his expression was genuine and kind.

'Come, lady. There is little time before we prepare for battle and I would see to your comfort first,' Brice said, waving off the other men. He held out his hand to her.

Gillian remembered being introduced to a number of them by name just after…just after she had spoken her vows, but they all blurred together. Now she tilted her head down and followed Brice away from the tent and into a small copse of trees that would shield her from the others as she sought privacy.

She tried not to think about the feelings and pleasure that the hand she now held had stirred within her just a short time ago. A tremor passed through her then, a reminder of the excitement and passion. Then, remembering the dismal end to it all, she shook her head and cleared her thoughts as she walked with him into the forest.

Considering her actions last night, she fully expected him to stay at her side, but thankfully he did not. He even managed to surprise her.

'Do you give me your word that you will not try to escape?' he asked.

'Escape, my lord? Now?'

'*Oui,* lady. Now,' he nodded. 'Do you give me your word you will not try to run…now?'

She thought on his words and realised that she had no place to run to, not now that he had claimed her as his wife. With her virtue intact, Oremund would have something to bargain with, but not now that she was no longer a virgin. Glancing up at him for a moment, she recognised the fact that he asked for her word and seemed willing to accept it in good faith was both unexpected and impressive. Gillian nodded without meeting his gaze again.

'Then you may enjoy a few minutes of privacy and I will wait for you at the tent, lady,' he said quietly before she heard his footsteps leaving.

Gillian nearly lost her balance as she realised she was truly alone there. Listening to the surrounding area, she could hear only the noises of the camp in the distance and nothing and no one close enough to stop her from leaving. The strangest part of it was that she could not raise within her the urge to run.

Rubbing her hands across her face, she knew that she was for ever different from the innocent girl who had sought refuge in the convent's walls. And though she did not feel like a true wife, the events of earlier this morn had made her one in the eyes of the law and the church. In spite of any denials she could muster, her heart, soul and body knew he had taken her virtue.

Sighing, Gillian finished seeing to her needs and began to walk back to his tent. She no longer had the opportunity of avoiding the coming battles or their outcomes. She could only pray that few lives would be lost in the struggle.

Chapter Six

His second-in-command and his squire, along with Stephen, stood blocking his path as he approached the tent. If their stances—arms crossed over the chests, legs spread wide in a fighting position—did not give him pause, their dark expressions did. Though Ernaut seemed nervous over such a confrontation, neither Stephen nor Lucais appeared to give it a second thought.

'What is the problem?' he asked, walking off the worn path and around them to reach the tent. 'I have not killed her or even left her for dead, if that is what you suspect,' he explained. Gillian might have knocked him unconscious and even escaped him last night, but this morn she was his wedded and bedded wife and more valuable in the upcoming battles than even his new destrier. They yet glared at him as he waited on an explanation for their mutinous behaviour.

'Speak of your concerns now or get back to your duties.' He owed them some measure of flexibility due to their shared past and friendships, but he was lord here and now would exercise that power even if they thought he would not.

The three men exchanged glances and finally Lucais stepped closer. Nodding at the tent, he asked, 'What happened between you and the lady, Brice?'

'The usual things that happen between a man and his wife,' he said through clenched teeth. His temper built—they had no right nor reason to question him on such personal matters. They knew, even as every man in the camp did, that he planned to make the marriage a true one last night. 'Why do you question me when you have no right to do so?' He crossed his arms over his chest, mirroring their stances.

Ernaut's colour ran high, his cheeks blushed and for a moment he appeared much younger than his four-and-ten years. He stuttered once, and then again, before motioning towards the tent with his hand. Brice turned to follow his gesture and spied the pile of bloodied rags on the ground there. Without thinking about the implications, he nodded and explained.

'I did not realise I'd spilled so much blood.'

The three men stared, their expressions now showing shock instead of understanding. Brice suddenly comprehended what they must think but had no chance to explain further for the woman in question walked towards them. He ordered them off with a jerk of his head, but they ignored him!

'My lady,' Ernaut began. 'The day is warming. Would you prefer to break your fast out here rather than in the tent?'

Watching the scene unfold, with all its misunderstandings, Brice fought the urge to laugh as he watched his men try to ease the lady's discomfort. He would disabuse them of their mistaken idea soon enough, but he allowed them to see to Gillian's comfort while he carried out other duties, all in preparation for their imminent assault on Thaxted Keep.

Later, when his belly growled in hunger, he realised that his squire had never returned with the lady or without her. And Ernaut had failed to return with his food, as well.

Brice walked towards the centre of the camp, to the place where several cooks oversaw the preparation of their food, such as it was while on military campaign, and soon heard her laughter echoing across to him. Following it, he found Gillian sitting on a stool, cushioned by several thick blankets, and surrounded by his men.

Being entertained by his men was a more apt description, for they stood around her, offering their names and their origins as well as the choicest bits of meat and cheese and even some fresh bread. For the first time, he had the chance to observe her from afar and to witness the way her eyes lit up as she smiled and enjoyed the simple pleasures of food and companionship.

He watched her lips curve enticingly as she spoke and teased Ernaut and his body responded once more to the mere thought of tasting her mouth and kissing her until she was breathless and moaning. And he wanted to thrash the young man for gaining her attention so.

And he noticed that she did understand their Breton tongue, for she laughed at some of the comments and questions from Ansel or Ernaut, and she stammered out a word or two in reply, as well. More surprises from the woman to whom he was now married!

But as he approached, he was noticed firstly by some of the men and then by the lady. They grew silent and wariness filled their gazes. Stephen, Ansel and Lucais lined up behind Gillian with Ernaut by her side, arms crossed and stances wide once more as Brice walked up to them. Rather than being threatened by such an action, he felt some relief at the sight of it.

If today, or in one of the other battles he yet faced, he fell, at least he now knew they would support her in her claim as his widow. Did Gillian know that she'd gained supporters, even against her rightful lord and husband? For now he would let this bond between them stand, even at the expense of his reputation as a man who had a care for women.

'If you have all broken your fast, there is much to be done and done quickly,' he called out. No matter what happened they would not sleep here this night.

The moment of silent challenge ended as the men strode away to finish loading their weapons on the wagons and closing down the camp, but not before offering a soft word or bow to his wife.

Lady Gillian stood after being abandoned by her protectors and, without saying a word as he watched, she found a bowl and filled it with the thick porridge that simmered in the cauldron near the fire. Walking up to him, she held it out.

'I do not think you have eaten yet, my lord,' she said as he took it. 'Ernaut has been busy seeing to my comfort when he should have seen to yours.'

She did not raise her eyes to meet his, but at least she'd stopped crying. Oh, he'd witnessed the tracks of tears on her cheeks as she walked into the forest earlier, in spite of her efforts to keep her face hidden. And the pit of his stomach had filled with bile because he knew he had caused them.

'My thanks, lady.' He nodded to her as he accepted the wooden bowl and spoon.

'A man must fill his belly before he goes into battle.'

Her tone was even, but he thought he detected something else there—anger, possibly, or even fear? Brice wondered what his men had revealed to her about his plans to take Thaxted from her brother.

'Just so, my lady,' he replied as he spooned some of the hot, though bland, porridge into his mouth.

He ate it all and ate it quickly, a habit of any man who'd travelled in a fighting force, for you never knew when or where or how the next meal might come. Though the king and his friend Giles had provided him with much support, including foodstuffs to last for a month-long siege if necessary, Brice could never break himself of the acquired practice.

She stood in front of him while he ate, watching everything his men did—taking down tents, packing up supplies, preparing weapons and horses without saying another word. Did she worry over her brother's fate? Or her own?

'Things have moved quickly over this last day and there is much we need to discuss,' he said, handing the empty bowl to one of the lads who helped the cooks. 'And we have not the time or proper place to hold those discussions,' he said, watching her face for some sign of...anything. 'I would like to leave you here, for your safety, but I need your presence to convince your brother to surrender.'

She laughed then, loudly and with a measure of some irony—an outburst he thought inappropriate—until she stopped abruptly. The lady met his gaze with an even expression, one that gave him no indication of her true feelings.

'My brother will not surrender because you hold me hostage, my lord. Indeed, he might even suggest ways of killing me.'

Brice could not be certain which shocked him more—the information she'd just shared or her nonchalant attitude about her brother's hatred towards her. 'Why would he act so dishonourably?'

The lady glanced away again, as she did each time her

brother became their topic. There was so much more going
on than he had time to discover.

'As you said, my lord. That discussion is best saved for another time and place.' She moved aside when two of his men
took the cauldron down from its hook and frame. 'I would be
willing to wait at the convent for you, my lord.'

Brice laughed then. 'You are persistent, lady,' he said with
a bow of his head. 'But, nay, your place is at my side now.' He
thought for a moment and asked her another question, one that
had confused him after hearing of her brother's resistance and
his hostility towards her.

'Your father's will named you to inherit this place. If you are
your father's heiress, and the king has given you in marriage
to me, how can your brother justify his fight?' Even a stubborn, stupid man would see that Brice had superior forces and
the legal right to the place now that Gillian was his wife.

'Regardless of the truth, my brother has always believed
that my mother bewitched my father into naming me as his
heiress. And since my brother is the only legitimate child born
to my father and his wife, many have agreed with him about
Thaxted and fight for his honour in this matter.'

Brice felt his mouth drop open and quickly closed it.
Apparently the bishop had not disclosed everything about the
lady to him after all. He could not think of a question or a comment to make even while he comprehended the many, many
possible problems in his plans and strategies to take Thaxted
that this revelation exposed.

He noticed then that she stared at him, most likely observing
and enjoying every moment of his discomfort over her origins.
The corners of that lovely, tempting mouth of hers threatened
to break into a smile, but she lowered her gaze and fought to

control it. He had no doubt that she had kept such information to herself intentionally, waiting for a good moment to use it.

As she just had.

'Ernaut!' he yelled loudly, loud enough to startle Gillian, who jumped at the sound of it. She'd just regained her composure when his squire came running.

'My lord,' the boy said, nodding his head in his own version of a bow. None of them had adjusted to Brice's new station or the respect due him now, not even he himself.

'Take the lady to my tent and see to getting things packed and ready to move,' he said, motioning for her to follow the boy. As Ernaut began to lead Gillian away, Brice grabbed his arm and pulled him close. 'Did you get rid of those…?' He did not finish.

Ernaut blushed and then nodded his answer and walked away. Gillian followed him, but continued to glance back until she disappeared around the curve of the path that led to his tent. Calling out to his closest friends, he went in search of Father Henry…and some answers.

Hours later, armoured and mounted and on the road to Thaxted, Brice knew he was no more certain of the way this would play out than he was when the lady revealed her true origins to him. Though the priest assured him that his claim was stronger than anyone else's, Brice understood more of Oremund of Thaxted's refusal to yield up the lands or keep. Oh, with the backing of the king any prior or future claims could be sustained or disregarded, but the cost of such fights would be high. Whether in men lost or in gold paid to those who now surrounded King William, insulating him from petitioners and benefiting from their positions.

Glancing back, he watched the lady riding between her new protectors. Though they kept their voices low, he could see them talking as they rode. She did not smile at him in that way. She did not initiate words between them. She… He let out a breath and shook his head. Turning back to face the road, he tried to focus on the coming battle.

It did not take long to reach the rest of his forces, camped not far from the walls surrounding Thaxted Keep. Between his own men and these he now led from his friend Giles and from the king, there should be no problem taking Thaxted.

He could not help but notice the expression of fear and concern on Gillian's face when he approached to help her from her horse and into a secure area out of sight from the walls. Those softer feelings he could understand—his newly wedded wife would stand by and watch her husband destroy her home and the last of her family. At least he would have understood those kinds of fears before she told him of the animosity between her and her half-brother.

Now, though, recognising the flicker of guilt that glimmered in her eyes, he worried over what other secrets she held and when they would be revealed.

Chapter Seven

Gillian almost felt sorry for the man.

His discomfort as his men saw the blood from his injury and mistook it for hers.

His confusion and anger over the way his men took her side and offered their support to her.

His complete shock at discovering that his wife was a bastard and had little claim on the lands and keep that he was trying to wrest away from her brother.

Pity welled up inside of her for those who would die in what would no doubt be a fruitless attempt to oust Oremund from the well-built, well-defended keep and manor.

Walking through Lord Brice's camp this morn, listening to and questioning his men and making her own estimates of his strength, all pointed to disaster when the battle against her half-brother and his allies began in earnest. Then, telling him of the futility of his claim, even with her as wife, worsened the situation and he'd not spoken a word to her since.

It had taken them only hours to retrace the steps of her journey from Thaxted, but when they reached the crest of the last hill and began to travel down, Gillian nearly lost her breath.

An army lay between them and Thaxted.

Easily twice the size of the group she now travelled with, they spread out around the manor like a second wall, preventing anyone from entering or leaving it. Searching the area near the northern part of the wall, she realised she would never have escaped if she'd waited another day.

The sounds of the men around her as they approached their comrades reminded her of her failure to escape. Then Brice strode towards her, his grim expression visible in spite of the helmet he wore, and apparent in every step he took. In more ways than one and in some he had no idea of, she'd become a liability to him and his plans to take Thaxted.

He reached up to assist her off the horse she'd been given to ride and his hands slid along her ribs until they rested below her breasts. Though he'd removed the metal gauntlets, he wore leather gloves underneath, which would most likely prevent him from feeling her, but that did not stop her skin from reacting. The tips of her breasts pebbled much as they did when he'd caressed them last evening.

With her hands on his shoulders, she met his gaze and watched as his brown eyes darkened to almost black. And in those eyes she saw the spark that told her that he'd recognised the way her body responded to such a touch. He allowed her to slide down him then, much more slowly than was needed to accomplish the task.

'We will do that when I am not wearing mail and armour, lady,' he promised in a husky whisper.

Apparently he was more pleased with their joining this morn than she'd been. Were men contented then with only a few moments of pleasure? From his passionate promise, it would seem that he intended to repeat the act again with her. Regardless of what she thought of their encounter, her body had other ideas and she felt a flash of heat pass through her when he stroked the undersides of her breasts as he waited for her to gain her balance.

Such heat tore through her that she nearly grabbed him to pull him close, before realising the meaning of such an action. Luck was with her, for the young Ernaut interrupted the moment and called to him.

'My lord?' he said quietly from just behind him. When Brice did not reply and did not move his heated gaze from hers, he called out more loudly then. 'My Lord Brice!'

He released her and stepped back so quickly that she nearly lost her balance once more. Before he turned to face his squire, he whispered a warning to her—one that surprised her for its wrongness and for his fervour.

'Think not to dally with my men. You are my wife and none of them will stand for you except by my orders.'

The only thing that kept her from breaking her hand was his quick reaction to the impulsive slap she tried to deliver in response to the insult to her honour. He grabbed it just as she began to raise it, saving her from further injury, but not from the pain of his accusation. When she tried to tug it free of his hold, he tightened his grip, a move that hurt and infuriated her.

'In the last day, I have been chased, taken prisoner, tied and bound, married against my will, had my virtue taken regardless of my own thoughts on the matter and now you insult me, my lord?' Using her other hand, she pried loose his fingers from around hers and stepped back, fearful she might be forced to try again to strike him. Gillian rubbed the one he'd held as she continued.

'I have managed to keep my virtue intact in spite of my brother's efforts to find someone to buy it or take it. I have fought off bigger and stronger men than yours to keep myself pure as I'd promised my father I would. Do you think that I would dishonour myself or my father's memory because you found a way to take it? Bastard or not, Saxon or not, I am no whore who will spread my legs for another!'

Gillian took a deep breath then, for her words had poured out so quickly and with such force she had not breathed while she spoke. She adjusted her veil and cloak in place and prepared to be led off and punished when she raised her head to find the reason for the spreading silence. She had not thought she'd raised her voice to the warrior, but apparently she'd been loud enough for those around them to hear.

His face took on a familiar appearance then, reminding her of Oremund when she'd pushed against his control or plans. Fury flashed in his eyes, followed by more rage and something else she couldn't identify. When he rested his hand on the hilt of his sword, she wondered if she now faced her death for such an outburst.

Beads of sweat gathered on her neck and back and began to trickle down under her gown. Breathing became difficult and Gillian sought for a way out of this humiliating and dangerous situation. Should she beg his forgiveness now? She wiped her damp palms against her gown. Should she submit to him in front of his men? Gillian shivered then, expecting orders for beatings or whippings at any moment. The silence drew out, making her shake with worry and anticipation.

Lord Brice broke the stalemate by looking away from her at those of his men closest to him. Lifting his hand from his sword, he removed his helmet and handed it to Ernaut, who stood in shocked silence at his side.

'I begin to understand why Oremund of Thaxted does not want her back.'

Deciding in that moment that this was not the time nor the way in which she wanted to die, she accepted his rebuke for what she knew it to be—a way to ease the terrible tension between them and to keep his dignity before his men. And as she'd learned early in life, men struck out when challenged or shown to be inferior. This time it had been with words and not blows. Gillian swallowed deeply and cleared her throat. Sinking into a low curtsy, one which nearly brought her to the ground, she submitted.

'Just so, my lord,' she began, trying to form an apology that would neither stick in her throat nor insult him further.

But her words were interrupted by his departure, for, as she remained low before him, he turned and walked away as though she mattered not. His men followed until there remained only her and Ansel.

'If you will come with me, my lady, I can take you to your tent.' He held out his hand to help her rise.

Gillian accepted it and rose from the curtsy, shaking and wobbling on her exhausted legs, brought on by riding all day after not riding for months, and spending that day trying to control and guide a lively horse who had more spirit than she had strength to rein it in. Ansel led her through the camp that now spread out even more with the addition of the men whom Lord Brice had brought with him.

They walked up away from Thaxted until they reached the edge of forest where the land inclined steeply, at so much of an angle that it prevented anyone from approaching the back of the tent raised there or from getting away in that direction.

Had he planned it that way because of her?

She might never know, for she was certain he was not done with her—with either her punishment or with his physical plans for her. And the fury she'd seen in his eyes matched or even surpassed that which she'd seen in Oremund's gaze after her last escape.

It had taken her a sennight to rise from her bed after that beating.

Ansel opened the flap of the tent and allowed her to enter first. Gillian looked around and saw that it was just as sparsely furnished as the other had been. Regardless of his new standing, Lord Brice saw himself as he always had—a penniless warrior fighting for his duke.

She sank down on the pallet, leaning against one of the supports for the tent and knew he would not return until much later to confront her. The only thing she knew for certain was that if he killed her he would never learn of the dowry her father had provided and hidden away before his death.

Penniless indeed, for what was hers now belonged to him as her lawful husband. If she could find it.

Lackwit.

A bloody lackwit.

A stupid, bloody lackwit.

Brice called himself every possible name he could think of that described the way he had completely lost control of himself, his anger, his thoughts, even his strategies and plans, since meeting the Lady Gillian of Thaxted a day ago.

Had it only been a day?

If this had only been a day, and he'd been tempted to tup, strangle or exile her a dozen times since meeting her, how would either of them survive a sennight…or a lifetime together? And since finding her traipsing along the road, running away from him, his body had suffered, his reputation had suffered and now even his mind had suffered.

Not to mention his pride.

Brice knew she'd not been satisfied during their joining. He'd decided to simply get the deed done and had failed to see to her pleasure. So because he sought expediency over her needs, her first experience with her husband, a man who had plenty of experience with the fairer sex, had been a disaster.

In spite of the way she'd challenged him before his men, he'd spent the entire day vacillating between lust and anger and pride and fear and just about every other reaction a man could have to the events he'd faced. But through it all, part of him just wanted to remove the guilt and fear from her eyes and to soothe the deep hurt she'd exposed unknowingly to him.

It was always easier, Sir Gautier had told them, to recognize your faults in someone else. And easier to place blame on others for your own shortcomings that you could not admit existed. Simon's father, who had fostered three bastards along with his own lawful son, had been a wise man and had shared that wisdom with the boys he raised.

As he walked from one end of the camp to the other, meeting the knights, foot soldiers and bowmen who would fight for him and his rights in the coming battle, he'd thought only of her. Twice he had to stop himself from going to their tent to check on her. And thrice more times he found himself standing and staring at her, as she'd convinced Ansel to allow her to remain outside the tent. At first, he thought to order her inside, for safety's sake, but then he noticed that she seemed to be enjoying the sun's warmth and the gentle breeze of the day. It was nightfall before he completed his plans and arrangements for the morning's attack and allowed himself to approach his tent.

Another guard stood in Ansel's place and nodded to him as he walked closer. Brice released a deep breath as he prepared to enter. The guard's whispered warning stopped him.

'The lady asked to speak to Father Henry, my lord. Ansel saw no reason to deny her request,' he explained. 'He only just finished shriving the men and arrived a few minutes ago.' The guard nodded at the tent, indicating that the priest was inside.

After handing his weapons and helm to the guard, Brice stood silently, unabashedly trying to hear some snatch of the conversation that was going on between his wife and the priest. He did not believe for a moment that a solemn confession of sins was the reason she'd summoned the old priest. And the words he could hear exchanged inside did not involve her sins or shortcomings, but his. He lifted the flap and entered, effectively ending their conversation in but a moment.

'My lord,' Father Henry said as he rose from the stool on which he sat. 'Come and join us.' The old man stepped aside and let Brice walk past to reach the lady. 'We were just speaking of you.'

Brice noticed the blush that crept up Gillian's cheeks and the guilty expression in her turquoise eyes that gave away the truth of the priest's words. With her veil drawn low over her forehead and the sides of her face, whether out of respect for the priest's presence he knew not, it was difficult to see much of her. 'Speaking about me, Father? And what have you told my wife of me?'

Before the priest could answer, the lady rose from her stool and spoke.

'My lord, I asked to speak to the good father because I remembered almost nothing from our wedding and I wished to confirm some details of our contract.'

Brice noticed she only met his gaze for a moment before staring past him or at her hands, but never at him. 'And was he able to answer the questions you had?'

'Aye, my lord,' she said, her voice so soft it was nearly a whisper.

'My lord,' Father Henry began. 'Brice.' He changed his address to a less formal one. 'Lady Gillian meant no disrespect to you by asking me.'

Brice frowned. Clearly both of them thought their discussion would anger him and feared his reaction. The lady, considering their encounter earlier, he could understand, but he'd done nothing to the priest or to anyone in his presence to warrant the kind of hesitation or concern shown now.

'And I took none from her requests to speak to you. Though I'd hope that she was seeking an opportunity to confess her sins and repent of them,' he said. He felt the smile curve the corner of his mouth and fought the urge to laugh aloud. She tilted her head back ever so slightly, but it was enough to see the now-familiar spark of anger in her eyes.

'My practice was daily confession, my lord. Until our priest left and I had none to hear mine.' The voice and tone were mild, but her eyes showed how she really felt.

He realised in that moment that he would rather have this angry and challenging wife than a solemn, frightened one. The fiery one who'd knocked him unconscious rather than the one who scraped the ground in obeisance at his feet earlier, not this one who felt the need to have a priest in the room to offer an explanation to him.

'Have you eaten yet, Father?' he asked. 'Would you stay to join us in our meal?' Ernaut entered, carrying a platter of sliced meats, cheeses and some bread.

The old priest looked from him to his wife and back again before saying a word. Brice could feel the powerful desire for her simmering in his blood, just beneath his skin, as it had since the moment he'd met her. Was it obvious to this man of faith? Could Father Henry tell Brice wanted nothing more than to peel off the lady's garments and have her beneath him for the rest of the night?

Father Henry cleared his throat and shook his head. 'Young Selwyn is seeing to my supper, my lord. But I thank you for your offer of hospitality.' He stood and walked to the entrance of the tent. 'Brice, if you would like, I can stay with Lady Gillian during...' the priest gave a worried glance at Gillian before continuing '...tomorrow.'

'I would value your company, Father,' the lady answered before he could. 'But I fear you will be needed in other places during the battle.'

To see to the wounded and the dying, Brice thought. They both turned their eyes to him and he nodded. 'I am certain that the lady will aid you in your work on the morrow, Father. She would seem to be the kind of woman who prefers to be working and busy rather than waiting.'

'I will leave you both then with a blessing.'

The priest lowered his head and mumbled words in Latin, ending with the Sign of the Cross over them. With a nod to him, Father Henry made his way out of the tent, leaving Brice to face his wife alone. He motioned for her to sit and partake of the food and drink Ernaut had set out on the small table for them. Without taking her eyes from his, she sat and waited for him. Brice poured some ale from the pitcher and handed her a cup.

They ate in quiet efficiency, but the tension between them grew stronger each second. When they each drank the last of their ale, Brice called for Ernaut to take away the platter and to help him out of his chainmail.

Once the boy left, Brice removed the quilted tunic and braes he wore under the metal protection and hung them in one corner of the tent to dry out before he needed them for the coming battle. Then he turned to face her, expecting that she would turn away and not watch him undress. He nearly smiled as her nerve returned, and for a moment he held her gaze.

Brice peeled off the undertunic, untied the loincloth he wore under the braes and loosened the garters around his legs. Turning his back to where she sat, he began washing as their breathing became the only sound in the room.

He glanced over his shoulder and found that she had looked away after all. He finished washing and leaned over for the length of drying linen. Wrapping it around his hips, he noticed the blush that filled her cheeks even though she was not looking at him. When she did turn towards him, he watched as her eyes opened wide, making them appear huge in her face. And her mouth, the one that he dreamt of all day, opened and closed as though she tried to speak, though no words would come out. Glancing down, he could see the evidence of his body's reaction to being so near to her and so naked with only a thin layer of linen between them. And so could she.

He had hardened again within minutes of being with her this morning and every glance or word she spoke or every sight of her caused it to remain like steel throughout the whole of the day. Now, the gaze of those bright eyes staring at him, at it, simply encouraged him to a larger, harder reaction.

Chapter Eight

The only thing that had kept her from falling was that she was seated at that moment. Gillian felt her cheeks grow hot and reached up to touch them. He'd undressed so quickly that she could not utter a word, not a word of protest or warning. This must be his usual habit, of removing the heavy chainmail and undressing to wash before sleeping, and he did not even seem to mind her presence.

Her body had reacted, though; her mouth had grown dry and her lungs could not seem to draw in a deep enough breath. Sweat formed on her neck and in the valley between her breasts. That place between her legs tingled, as did the tips of her breasts. She pushed herself to her feet and almost ran to the opening of the tent.

Gillian wanted nothing so much as a cold cloth to place on her face, to ease the spreading heat in her cheeks, but he held the only washing cloth in the tent. He finished and wrapped a towel around his waist and handed the bowl of dirty water outside to Ernaut, issuing hurried instructions in a low voice. Then he spoke to her.

'Ernaut will bring fresh water for your use, lady. Do you have need of anything else before seeking your rest?'

Mayhap it was the undertone in his voice, or the pure masculine appeal of his well-formed, well-muscled body there naked before her, or just her complete and unseemly interest in the physical part of marriage, but whatever the reason, the urge to pull her cloak free and unlace the ties that restricted her breathing and kept the heat in place almost overwhelmed what little common sense she possessed in that moment.

'Nay,' she managed to say, shaking her head and clenching her hands against her cloak.

He shivered then, his skin turning to gooseflesh. 'Does it ever warm here in your England? The coldness is enough to shrink a man's…' He laughed aloud then and frowned as though searching for a different word from the one she knew he wanted to say. 'After spending a winter here, I long for the lands in Brittany without this relentless cold and dreariness.'

'Mayhap you should dress then, my lord?' she suggested, accepting the bowl of steaming water brought in by Ernaut. The redness creeping up the boy's face along with the immediate silence in the tent told her of her error in thinking. Clearly, Lord Brice had no intention of dressing. Ernaut coughed several times and backed out of the tent without meeting her surprised gaze again.

Lord Brice did not speak again to her, either. He organised his garments and boots and sword, ones he would wear on the morrow no doubt, and then walked over to the pallet in the corner. When she dared a glance in his direction, he seemed oblivious to her presence. But when she'd finished washing and was herself ready to sleep, she found him lying with his arms behind his head, simply watching every move she made. The towel that had offered a small amount of decency after that shocking display of his body lay crumpled on the floor next to the pallet and that meant he now lay naked under the blankets.

Gillian waited and waited for him to break the tension, to tell her where to sleep or what he expected, but he did not. Finally, she tried to be bolder than she felt.

'I know not what you expect from me, my lord,' she said, hearing her voice tremble.

He smiled then, one that lifted the corners of his mouth and made him appear younger and less formidable, but no less attractive. He lifted the blankets, exposing more of himself to her.

'Come to bed.'

'I am not ready to sleep,' she replied, more awake now than she'd been before. The images of his skin and the memories of the way he'd touched and kissed her beneath the blankets last night and this morning flooded her then, making sleep the last thing she thought on.

'Come to bed,' he repeated. His smile grew wicked and he tempted her to climb under the blankets with him. Her body understood the invitation more than her mind and she felt the heat spread throughout her as he held the covers higher.

'I do not know what you expect of me,' she repeated quietly, her usual confidence torn apart by the changes in her life this last day. Once more, and with a suddenness that surprised her, tears burned and threatened to fall. He sat up, drew his knees closer to his chest and leaned his arms there.

'In these hours before dawn, I seek only some comfort in the arms of my wife.' His expression gave away nothing more than his words did. 'If I live through the coming battle, we will find our way through the rest of it.'

Though not innocent any longer, Gillian did not know how

to approach this stranger who was her husband. With her syrce and cyrtel still on and her cloak covering her from neck to feet, she could not imagine what he expected of her now. Did husbands simply toss up the skirts of their wives as they did their lemans or serving women? Was it not different somehow?

'Take off your cloak and join me here, lady,' he said in a voice so deep and husky with emotion that it made her breasts tingle. 'Or is it your custom to sleep in such garments?'

Truth be told, aye, sometimes she needed to sleep in as many layers of clothing as possible, for comfort or for safety, but he did not need or want to know such things now. 'Not my cloak,' she said, probably revealing more than she should have. He frowned at her reply before she shook her head and stopped him from asking more. 'Nay, my lord.'

'Brice,' he said, sliding back and holding the blankets higher again. 'Call me by my name when you come to my bed.'

Deciding that some courage would be needed to get herself onto the pallet and into his arms, Gillian closed her eyes and dropped her cloak on the ground at her feet. Tugging her veil loose, it followed. Then, before she could hesitate, she pulled her cyrtel and syrce over her head and dropped them, as well, leaving her naked but for her shoes and stockings, and shivering from the coldness in the tent. Her skin pebbled quickly and she felt the tips of her breasts tighten from it.

'Lady,' he said, inviting her once more.

She capitulated, whether from the coldness of the tent or the warmth of the invitation she knew not, but she knelt down on the pallet and found herself in his embrace a moment later. He encircled her with his strong arms, drew her down next to him and pulled the thick layer of blankets over their bodies.

Feigning a bravery she did not yet feel, Gillian tried to ease the tension between them. 'And you should call me Gillian when you are in my bed.'

He drew back and looked at her, as though he could not believe her words. 'Just so, Gillian,' he replied. Then he dipped his head, touching his mouth to hers, and she forgot words and names and nearly how to breathe.

From frightened woman to bold one, Gillian had changed right before his eyes. He'd recognised the fear of an innocent in her gaze when he undressed and washed in front of her. But then, as he gave her time and space, she seemed to relax in his company and allow herself to accept what had happened and what would happen between them. Her admission that she did not know what to do touched him, for it revealed a vulnerability she most likely guarded from others.

Now, as he pulled her under him and plundered her mouth the way he'd been dreaming of all day, he knew that he must— nay, he wanted to make this night special for her. As special as last night had not been. And special enough for her to remember if it was their last night.

She opened to him, but left her hands resting at her side and not touching him. So he reached over and guided one to his waist. As he touched and tasted the heated depths of her mouth, he felt the other hand slide along his skin to rest on his hip. His hardness surged then against her leg. Brice lifted his mouth and trailed kisses down her neck and onto her shoulders. When she shifted against him, her hips against his erection, he slipped his hand lower and laid it on her belly.

Slow and easy was his motto this night; even if it killed him, he would bring her to pleasure before seeking his. Her innocent reactions to his kiss and his caress made it nearly impossible, as did the blood pounding through his veins and the hunger she caused within him. His erection grew stronger and he rubbed it against her, enjoying the friction. Not as pleasurable as the touch of her hand or the tightness of her womanly flesh would be, but for now, it would suffice.

Brice discovered that Gillian's breasts were very sensitive, so he leaned over and kissed her there. Then he laved the nipples until they grew taut. Drawing one into his mouth, he tongued the tip and then nipped at it with his teeth. Her gasp and shallow breaths told him to continue, but her hands holding his head there demanded it of him. And he complied, smiling against her soft skin and teasing each side equally.

When she moved mindlessly against his hand and he was nearly out of control, he slipped his fingers between her legs and found that place to be wet and hot. At first touch, she held her legs tightly together, but as he rubbed firmly, then softly, and as he slid his fingers deeper inside the heated folds there, her legs fell open and he could caress her more fully. And he did.

Soon, she trembled beneath his hands and his mouth. Lifting his head, in spite of her disgruntled moans when he did so, he kissed her mouth again, stroking inside and finding her tongue and suckling on it. With stronger and stronger motions, he brought her to the edge of her pleasure and pushed her over. Knowing that this was new to her, he urged her on.

'Let go, Gillian. Let your body go,' he whispered to her, never ceasing or easing up on the movements of his hand between her legs.

When he felt the first quivers of tightening within her begin, he opened the folds of her nether lips and touched the tiny bud there. Her reaction was immediate and well worth his efforts. She clutched at his shoulders as the pleasure struck her, her body shuddering and trembling in his grasp, so he continued until she shook less and less, but moaned deeply in her throat. Then he felt her body relax in his embrace and she opened her eyes. Confusion filled them as she gazed at him.

'What happened?' she asked in a whisper. Still panting, she pushed some of the loosened tendrils of her hair from her eyes.

'That is pleasure,' he said softly. 'Have you never experienced it before?'

Though she'd been a virgin, there were ways to enjoy the pleasures of the flesh that did not include piercing a maidenhead. He'd done so many, many times with women who sought to have him in their beds.

Her body trembled once more as a final wave shot through her and his body hardened in response. She noticed, for she gasped at the movement against her hip.

'You did not...' she began. 'You have not...'

'Not yet,' he said, gritting his teeth against the need to fill her with his hardness.

'Why not? I thought you wanted to seek...comfort.'

He rolled away from her for a moment. Talking about what he wanted to do while close enough to do it and while trying not to was far too difficult when he could feel the heat of her skin and the way her heart still beat at the faster pace her passion had caused. Whatever words he thought to say vanished as she rolled onto her side and faced him.

'Do you need help? I would think that to repeat the...act of this morning so soon must be difficult,' she asked in one breath. At first he thought her to be joking, but the serious and concerned glint in her eyes told him she was sincere in asking. 'What must I do to aid you?'

He was in heaven and in hell, for his newly wedded wife was a temptress who knew not her own appeal. And who had little real knowledge of what went on between men and women. Brice would offer thanks later to have such a woman, but for now he tried to remember how to speak when all he wanted to do was climb over her lush, naked body and plough it as deep and hard as he could and forget what the coming dawn could mean to each of them.

'Touch me.'

It was all he could say.

He closed his eyes and stopped breathing as she raised her hand and reached out towards him. Waiting to feel the first touch of her hand filled him with an anticipation not usual to him. Then her fingers grazed over his own nipples, causing them to pucker beneath her touch as her own had under his.

'Did that hurt?' she asked softly. He noticed she did not stop as she asked, sliding her fingers across his skin and touching the other one.

'Nay,' he groaned out, wanting, needing her to touch another part of him and praying she would not.

Then she curled her fingers and let her hand glide down over his chest and across his stomach. She tickled the curls of hair there, but stopped before touching his erection. It reacted as though she had and he could not stop his body from arching against hers. But she did not touch, moving on to slide her fingers along the length of his thigh and back again.

He used his free hand to take hers and place it where he truly wanted it, unable to resist the temptation any longer. Gillian's eyes widened and her mouth opened, provocatively so, as she encircled his cock and closed her grasp around it. It was his turn to gasp as she moved her hand along the length of him and then down again.

Just when he believed her capable of bringing him to release in this manner, for she was effective no matter how awkward or inexperienced her movements were, she released him. Brice might have begged in that moment of mindless pleasure, he could not be certain, but he tried to rein in his growing desire and need for her and let her lead...for now.

'You look in pain,' she whispered.

Though she'd released him, she continued to slide her hand over his skin, touching his stomach and his thighs and his chest in slow, languid caresses that did nothing to soothe the tension inside of him. He doubted that she had any awareness of the resultant desire spinning nearly out of control in him.

'I want you, Gillian,' he growled then. 'I want you now.'

She smiled then and it lit her face and eyes with a glimmer that was angelic and bedevilling at the same time and one that he would dream about in the coming days and years. 'Have me then, my lord,' she said, in a low whisper. 'Brice,' she corrected.

He must like boldness in women, for he laughed at her words and then kissed her with such ferocity that she felt the passion in him make her toes curl. A pulsing desire began to unfurl within the deepest part of her, not yet calmed from his earlier attentions. Now that she'd felt the pleasure he'd given, her body wanted it again, even if it meant enduring the other part of the act that was not as good. And while she knew that the next morn all their complications would need to be faced, she decided that this night was for them...and for this.

She gasped then as he released her mouth and lifted her leg over his hip. That hot place between her legs felt the cool air of the tent, but he did not wait for long to show her another route to pleasure. Soon, she could not stop her body from arching into his hand. He used his fingers against that sensitive place and made her even hotter within moments. Gillian tried to touch him again, but he would not let her, guiding her hand instead to rest on his leg. She feared he would have nail marks in the skin there, for it was difficult not to clutch and scratch him as her body ached for more.

When he moved between her legs and she found herself on her back beneath him, she tried to enjoy the waves of pleasure moving through her. She watched as he threw his head back and positioned himself to enter her, clearly something more pleasant for a man than a woman. Closing her eyes then, she tried to make her body remember the peak to which he'd driven her, for she knew it would be over very soon.

And then he filled her with his hardness and she could not breathe or move or think.

Instead of pain there as before, she could now feel the length and width of him as he moved inside of her, sliding in deep and then drawing out. The same throbbing, needful ache returned and soon her hips rose to meet his thrusts. He guided her legs up around his waist and then leaned down on his arms, keeping himself so close that she could feel the curls on his chest tickling and teasing her breasts.

And it was wonderful.

'Better this time?' he asked, his pause only a slight hesitation before moving deeper and deeper still.

'Aye,' she replied. It was all she could utter at that moment.

Her body needed no words, for her blood pounded again and her heart beat so quickly she could hear it and feel it in her ears. As he thrust into her, her woman's core tightened around him and something swirled in the centre of her body, making her inner muscles clench around his hardness to keep him there. Hot sweat beaded on her skin and tracked down her neck and back, and Gillian could not form a coherent thought in her head. His body pushed hers into such a state of excitement that she shuddered and shook at every move or touch or caress.

Gillian heard him urging her on to something, but her body responded without her control, seeking that peak that she'd found the first time alone, but now with him. She clutched at his powerful back, holding on tightly as she felt his length within her surge and pulse. Her body seemed to answer it by reaching her peak and feeling wave after wave of a pleasure she'd never known had existed.

Brice stopped then, his face straining and his arms shaking under his weight and his exertions. After a few minutes, he opened his eyes and met her gaze.

'Are you well?' he asked.

Gillian had no answer, for her heart pounded and tremors flowed through her from the pleasure. Taking a breath and releasing it, she sighed. 'I know not.'

He laughed then and kissed her quickly before withdrawing and moving to her side. 'A far better showing than this morn's attempt, I think,' he said, his voice exuding a masculine pride any woman would understand.

Even more, she understood why he had been driven to do this now, when so many more important things needed to be done and said between them.

First, Gillian knew that men's lust rose just before and after battles and the need to couple increased at those times, too. She'd seen it happen enough times to know about it.

Also, she knew that this man, her husband, had a certain reputation regarding his past liaisons. That bit of gossip she'd overheard while in the camp, from some of the other women who'd followed their men to England. A beautiful man who drew women to his bed like flies to honey and who never slept alone. A man who never left a woman unsatisfied, though until now she had had no idea of what that meant. So making certain that he tended to his wife as well as he tended to other women was important to him—and to his reputation.

He guided her to her side and moved up against her, his flesh on hers, sharing the heat of his body in this cold night. Just as she sank into sleep's grasp, she realised another reason why he'd pursued such pleasure and comfort in her arms.

Brice accepted that he could die on the morrow.

Chapter Nine

Gillian awoke with a start. For a moment she could not remember where she was, but then her body, aching in places unknown only a day ago, reminded her.

She lay abed with her husband.

A Breton knight with hopes of taking Thaxted from her brother.

A bastard knight gifted her by his king.

A man who had given her such pleasure that it nearly took her breath and ability to think away.

Nearly, for in thinking about those exact events between them since she had joined him in his bed, she could have never imagined so many different ways to offer or receive pleasure. Though the first time had been at a somewhat even pace, the other times he took her were not. Once he even entered her from behind, caressing her breasts, and that place between her legs, as he moved inside her.

And the last time. She closed her eyes, remembering that the last time had been so powerful and fast and deep that she thought she might have fainted at the end of it. They'd both drifted off to sleep then, exhausted from their joinings and their day.

She could hear the sounds of the rousing camp readying for battle. Gillian turned over to look at him, wondering how he would greet her or speak to her or look at her after such intimacies as they'd shared, but found an empty spot next to her on the pallet.

Holding the blankets against her, Gillian sat up and looked around the tent. Her own garments lay across the bottom of the pallet while his were gone. She listened for a moment and then tugged her syrce and cyrtel on before anyone could enter and find her naked. In a few minutes, her veil and cloak were in place and she lifted the flap of the tent.

But she found the camp nearly empty.

Had she slept through the battle? Surely she could not have! Obviously, Brice thought her secure in his tent and left without waking her, but a battle would be too noisy to miss. Realising that he expected her to be with Father Henry, she set off to find him. Wending her way through the assembled tents, she knew from watching yesterday that the priest was located towards the eastern end of the encampment and, with the help of a few servants and women, she headed there immediately.

Though she'd never been this close to a battle before, Gillian could not believe one could be this quiet. Then she realised that the deathly silence extended towards the walls of Thaxted. Shielding her eyes from the sun, she peered across the camp and found row after row of armed soldiers lined up around her keep. Without realising it, she walked in that direction until stopped by the priest whom she sought.

'Lady Gillian, come with me,' he said. Taking her arm, he tugged her back. ''Tis not safe for you there.'

'Has it begun then, Father?' she asked, not ready to seek

the safety of the back when too many she knew were at the front of the attack.

'Nay, my lady,' he said, shaking his head. 'Your brother and Lord Brice are speaking.'

'About me? About my lands?'

Before he even replied, she realised her error—the lands did not belong to her any longer, nor did she have any rights now. Both belonged to the man she married. These Normans had a different opinion about the position and rights of women, different from those of England or Wales or Scotland, and even the Norse who'd controlled parts of it until only recently. To a Norman, everything belonged to the man.

But so conveniently for their aims, they would uphold her father's will by giving the lands to her while then entrusting its control and powers immediately to her husband.

'They speak of peace and an amicable solution to this confrontation instead of one that will cost both men in lost lives, my lady.' Father Henry had spent many years negotiating with enemies; it was clear to her from his soothing tone and choice of words.

'And I am to play no part in these discussions?' she asked.

She could only imagine what lies her brother would tell him. And worse, the accusations he would make against her and her mother. Oremund would say or do anything to finally get control over Thaxted and anything necessary to find where their father had hidden his fortune. Though, certainly, he would never mention the existence of it to her Breton husband.

'Indeed, lady,' the very man said from behind her. Whirling around, she found Brice and two of his commanders standing there.

This was not the man who'd whispered endearments in a deep voice as he touched her most private places. This was not the man who pushed her, body and soul, to pleasure she'd not dreamed of. This was not a man...this was...the king's warrior.

Gillian had seen him in his chainmail and armour, his hauberk and helm and with his sword at his side. She'd witnessed him in command of his men on the road when she'd hidden in the forest. She shuddered as he approached, tempted to move closer to the priest. As though a mere man of God would thwart him in whatever his intentions were!

'Your brother wishes to speak to you and make certain you are well and safe. He has been searching for you for days and heaps praise on the Almighty that you were not harmed in your foolish journey,' he said evenly, while his gaze turned darker and more intense. He spoke through clenched teeth and she watched as the muscles in his jaw tightened.

Two men stood next to him and did not move or speak and Gillian felt sure that they were going to drag her off and hand her over to her brother. Suddenly her confidence was shaken and she feared saying anything to him about her brother's true intentions. Considering her earlier thoughts on Brice's possible duplicity, silence might be her best option.

Though it was never her practice.

'And you believe him, my lord?' She crossed her arms over her chest, challenging him, she knew, but he needed to understand how her brother lied. 'You would take his word over mine?'

He watched as her eyes flashed with angry fire and the way she held her body screamed out the defiance she clearly felt. Much as she'd thrown herself into the passion they'd shared, now she was ready to defend herself to him with everything in her. But at this crucial moment, he could not allow it.

Although Brice knew her brother to be a scheming liar who would sell his mother to the devil to get what he wanted, any sign that he was being swayed by Gillian would undermine his position right now. A man bowing and scraping to his wife of one day would be seen as weak, and he could not allow that.

'He is a man, after all, lady,' he said, not answering her question, but not denying it. Her face turned red and he thought she would explode, but instead her eyes narrowed for a moment and she met his gaze. Staving off more questions, he motioned for her to follow his men.

Father Henry moved as though to step between Gillian and him. Brice had seen the old man do the same thing in Taerford, mediating between the lord and his lady several times. But coming now, it could bring about a bad ending to his plans.

'You have no reason to be concerned about the lady's safety, Father,' he said. 'She is my wife.' The lady in question turned back to face him.

'So you will defend my rights against my brother's attempt to take them from me?'

He felt the pull on the corners of his mouth and fought a remarkable urge to laugh. No matter that he admired most everything he discovered about her, he could not show approval. 'You mean my rights, Lady Gillian, do you not?' He reached out and took her hand, tugging her to his side. 'Now that I control everything you brought to this marriage.'

Brice thought she might dig her heels in, but she capitulated and walked at his side. At least, she would be near him and he could protect her from anything that happened. His heart calmed from its rapid beat and he thought about the scenarios that could play out before them this day.

When he'd returned to the tent and found her gone, he'd nearly shouted out her name. His meeting before dawn had drawn him away for a short time and he expected to be there when she woke. Instead, he was met by an empty bed and a missing woman. His first thought was that she'd escaped again. Then he forced the rational part of himself to examine that likelihood.

When he remembered that she'd told the priest she would help him this day, Brice knew where she'd gone and his irritation at her making him worry for even a moment boiled over in his greeting. Now, he wanted to reassure her, but dared not. She was an intelligent woman, she would understand when he had the chance to explain it to her.

Surely she would.

They'd nearly reached the open field where his men stood ready when she tugged her hand from his and walked by herself.

Mayhap she would not.

As he'd told her last evening, there were many things to be sorted out between them once this day was done. Now was not that time.

They walked back through the rows of tents and soon approached the lines of men waiting to fight. Her confident stride faltered and she surprised him again when she held out her hand to him.

'Is there no other way?' she whispered.

'Your brother said that he would turn the keep over to you once he knew you were safe and this was your choice.'

Gillian stopped so suddenly that he took three paces before

he realised it. Turning back, he found her standing with an in-credulous expression fixed on her face.

'Gillian, there is no time for this. Men's lives are at stake here,' he warned.

'He is a liar.' Crossing her arms over her chest, she chal-lenged him yet again. Leaning over, she lowered her voice so that only he could hear her words. 'He is a poxed, degenerate liar and a man not worthy of your trust.'

Suspecting what he did while knowing even less, Brice could not reveal what he'd learned about her brother and his plans.

'And you have been trustworthy? Tell me how?' He took a step towards her, closing any space between them. 'Was it when you hid from my efforts to find you? Or when you lied about who you were? Or mayhap I should trust you because you knocked me unconscious and fled? Upon which of those trustworthy moments between us should I rely for making such a judgement of you?'

Her lovely face blushed and she looked away, not meeting his gaze. Their start had not been the best, but Brice believed it could be good between them—once he claimed his lands and took control of them. Giles had not had an easy time of it and they knew their grants were among the choicest in the land. Some of the most dangerous to claim, but the choicest still.

'Come,' he said more quietly, 'your brother waits on you.'

She said nothing more as he led her to the open field that separated them from her home and her brother's forces. Her brother and two of his men sat mounted on their horses and watched just as silently. The flag of truce at his side was the only reason Brice had not already cut him to pieces.

His men expected a trap of some kind and their alertness

was palpable to him. Lucais, Stephen and the others in charge
of sections of his fighting forces all watched carefully for his
signals and for anything out of the ordinary. Plans had been
made and put in place so that by the end of this day, he would
be lord of Thaxted in name and in fact.

'Ah, dearest Gillian,' Oremund called out. 'You are safe and
sound!' He dismounted and held out his arms to her. 'Come,
let me greet you as a brother should greet his dearest sister.'

Brice noticed that Oremund's smile did not reach his eyes
and that Gillian did not move from his side. 'The lady stays
here until our business is settled, Oremund.'

The only trait he could see in common between the two
siblings was the colour of their hair, so Gillian must resemble
her mother more than their common father.

'I have given you my word, Lord Brice. Do you not trust
me to stand by it?'

The man frowned and waited for his reply. Brice could feel
Gillian's tension. He glanced at her to try to gauge what she
was thinking. She said nothing, and stared forwards at her
brother.

'Your dead king gave his word to my king, as well,
Oremund.'

Not a denial and not an outright insult, but close enough to
make certain he was not taken for a fool. The son of Eoforwic
nodded his understanding.

'Sister, Lord Raedan wishes to know if you entered this
marriage of your own choice or if you've been forced to it,'
Oremund said evenly.

Brice placed his hand on the hilt of his sword. From
Oremund's wary expression Brice knew he understood how
close he was to drawing it in answer to the insult, but he had

sworn to Oremund that he would not interfere with Gillian answering any question put to her.

'I—' she began, until Oremund waved her off.

'Whatever has happened, whatever poor decision you may have felt compelled to make, Lord Brice has given his word to release you from it.'

Brice felt her surprise and nodded to her, even though he had absolutely no intention of letting her go. Let them both think what they wanted—she was his. But giving her this chance to disavow her promises was like opening a window into the way she thought and that would be valuable to him in the days to come. She stared at him while her brother continued, and he could get no impressions from the now-empty look in her eyes.

'So, Gillian, do you seek release from your situation?' her brother asked again.

His men shifted restlessly behind them. Very few would understand the reasons behind his actions, but none would question him. At least not now, though from the glares of several of his commanders, there would be questions later.

'No.'

Her reply was shocking and simple and not what her brother expected of her, but then he never had understood her. Gillian was not certain that Lord Brice did, either, but he'd done nothing yet that made her feel as terrified as her brother did. And though she'd like to be free of the control of men, she knew that was not the way of the world and would never happen. Since she had said the words, since she'd witnessed honour within him even when she provoked the worst in him, Gillian decided to truly cast her fate in with his.

'Think on your words carefully, sister,' Oremund warned

in that silky smooth tone he used when others were listening. 'The fate of your people, your family, lies in the balance here.'

Another threat disguised as concern. So many of her people had been run off by Oremund or sold off as William the Conqueror's forces and the ravages of a harsh winter without a fruitful harvest rolled across the land. The once thriving keep and village now withered under Oremund's harsh hand. And with her mother dead these last years and her uncle able to defend himself, she worried not for them. So lost in her thoughts and all the arguments she could make, Gillian realised they waited on her.

'Lady Gillian, what say you to your brother's question?'

Would he, Lord Brice, really let her go? Had she misinterpreted everything he'd said and everything she knew of him? There was not time to consider all the implications of his decision, but she'd already made hers and for reasons both practical and irrational.

'No,' she repeated. 'Oremund, I stand by the vows I took.'

Gillian had no idea how much she shook or how nervous she was until Brice walked closer and stood behind her. He placed his hands on her shoulders and she felt his strength.

'Well done,' he whispered in her ear as he pulled her against him. 'Well done.'

Had he doubted her? Had he planned this to justify his actions in attacking Thaxted? Did he really believe that she could have given herself with such abandon through the night and then walked away from him in the light of the morn? Gillian sensed so much more beneath and behind what she could observe and hear. Something much bigger than her own aims was at stake.

Gillian felt that something deep within her trusted her husband and she accepted the certainty that she was safer with him than at the questionable or non-existent mercies of her brother. But were his words truly showing his approval of her declaration?

Oremund lost control then and everyone there saw the man she usually dealt with—dangerous, poisonous, selfish and attacking. Luckily, men with very big swords stood between them this time.

'You traitorous, lying bitch!' he screamed, his face contorted with rage. He took two steps towards her, but a wall of armoured warriors formed, keeping him at bay. 'You will pay for this betrayal.'

She knew she'd backed away and pressed herself more firmly against Lord Brice. For the first time, she'd felt safe in the face of her brother's rage. More importantly, she knew this was not the end for his habit was to strike out verbally first and then use other methods to apply punishment for perceived slights or offences. When it was clear he would not get closer to her, he strode to his horse, mounted it and rode off towards the keep.

This was not the end of it.

Gillian turned to warn Brice. He had no true idea of how dangerous Oremund could be when enraged like this. He released her as she moved and she found him looking pleased beneath his helm. And as she looked from one to another of his men, she found the same expression on all of them!

'This is not over, my lord!' she exclaimed in a voice kept low so that only he heard her. 'He will not give up Thaxted without a fight. It was only a—'

'A ploy, lady. Aye, I never expected him to walk away,' Lord

Brice replied. 'Ernaut, take Lady Gillian back to Father Henry and stay there,' he ordered as he mounted his own horse.

'My lord,' both she and Ernaut spoke at the same time.

But Brice was already thinking about the coming battle and had given them an order that he expected them to obey without question or hesitation. Just as the men behind her began to move into their position, she realised that she could stop the battle now. Or at the least, she could reduce the number of dead at the outcome. Gillian ran over to him and reached out to touch his leg, to gain his attention.

'My lord,' she called out over the growing noise of men preparing to fight. 'My lord, I must speak with you.'

He frowned at her and motioned with a nod of his head for her to move off. She did not, for she knew if she told him about the passage under the keep, he could enter it and take the stronghold. When he realised that she would not move away, he leaned over towards her.

'There is another way—'

The bolt hit her before she could finish and the force of its impact in her shoulder drove her to the ground. Searing, tearing pain coursed through her and her head began to swirl. Her stomach gripped and rolled within her as the pain reached a level she'd never endured.

Chaos ruled the day then and she could only hear the shouting get louder and louder and she fell further and further from it all. Everything around her blended together—the light of the sun, the wind that moved through the trees, Brice ordering them to set the arrows aflame and burn the keep to the ground.

Oh, dear God, no! She must stop him. Gillian watched as he approached, fierce and angry, calling out orders with each step until she was too dizzy to focus her eyes on him. He lifted her as though she weighed nothing and began to carry her away from the confusion.

'My lord,' she said, weakening with every breath she took.

'Hush now, Gillian,' he whispered against her forehead. 'Father Henry will see you to rights.'

'Brice! Stop!'

He paused then and her vision began to blur. Blood now soaked her clothing and she could not feel her arm. Gillian tried to squint to see his face, but she could not.

'Brice, I can show you a way in. There is no need to burn it down,' she begged. 'I pray thee, please, my lord. There are innocents in there who will perish with the rest.'

Though he did not say it, she continued on, forcing out the words as the darkness called to her. 'Forty paces from the north wall...a stand of trees... At the bottom of the middle one...' she shook her head to clear it, but wisps of fog surrounded her '...when you climb through, you will be at the back of the smith's cottage.'

Gillian reached for him then, but could not feel him. 'Promise me you will let them live.'

She never heard his answer, but the shout that he made echoed in her head and she felt it as she fell against his chest. Then, the day faded to black and it was over.

Chapter Ten

Brice felt her faint and in a way it was better than having her awake. The arrow had pierced her high in the shoulder area, probably more flesh wound than real damage, and simply confirmed to him what a miserable cur her brother was.

Shooting his own sister in the back!

Oremund had sunk to a deeper low than any man he'd known—first abusing Gillian and then punishing her for her resistance. It was obvious to him that Oremund could have and would have killed her long ago unless she held some value to him. Oh, the sentiment of close relatives meant nothing to him, but the monetary or power kind did, otherwise the bastard daughter would have followed her mother and father in death, with little notice or fanfare to mark it. That meant Gillian had something that Oremund wanted. Something she'd escaped from Thaxted with. And since she had brought next to nothing with her but the clothes on her back, it must be some information she held.

He held her closer and walked quickly through the lines to the camp where word of her injury had already spread. Two of the men who saw to injuries directed him to a cot where he laid her on her side so she did not rest on that shoulder. Father Henry ran over to them and knelt at her side.

'How did this happen?' he asked.

''Twas always his plan, I think. To intimidate her. To punish her.' He'd felt the scars on the backs of her legs and on her hips and buttocks when they'd made love. Brice knew that scars like that came from frequent beatings. Dear God in heaven! What had she endured under Oremund's control? No wonder she tried to escape every time she could.

Once Gillian was being attended, Brice returned to the front of his forces. She had offered him a way in that would enable him to spare the keep and most of those inside. Though he cared not if Oremund lived or died, the others living there would eventually be the ones to tend his lands. Alive was much better than dead or maimed.

His men were not happy when he revealed the change in plans. Once the excitement of the approaching battle began to rouse a man's blood, it was difficult to simply walk away. He could feel it stirring in his own veins, but he suspected that part of what he felt was rage over Gillian's injury. He should never have allowed her that close to Oremund. He should have ignored all the bluster and kept to his own plan and she would never have been there to be shot. His failure could have cost her life, and it might yet, if infection set in or if it did not heal well.

Lucais and Ansel argued against his new plan, but he watched as Stephen and Richier, experienced warriors both, considered it and nodded. They all offered to be part of the small group sent through the tunnel or passage into the keep. They left to make their preparations and he made arrangements for the diversion to occur to draw attention to the front wall and away from the opening.

Brice decided that letting some time pass before the attack was a good strategy—his men knew the plan, but those inside most likely expected an immediate attack in retribution. It was possible that Gillian's plea had saved the lives of many in the keep and in his own lines, for running into a battle fuelled by anger was dangerous. War was something best met head on with cold resolve and cool-headed focus.

And they did so, later that day, with a focused efficiency learned from fighting together many times in many places against various enemies. He'd trained and fought with the men he'd selected as his commanders in Brittany, in Normandy and now in England, and would trust them with his life.

The only thing Brice lamented was the lack of his two closest friends at his back. The last missive from Giles, written in his own hand at that, promised his presence as soon as Lady Fayth gave birth. The news of Soren was promising and distressing at once—he continued to recover from his injuries received at Hastings, but was a changed man from the one they knew. The 'beautiful bastard', the name by which he was called and known because of his looks, a name and appearance that gave him entry into the beds of many desirable women, was gone. The grievous wounds of battle had taken their toll on his appearance and his soul, it would seem.

Brice's men performed as he expected—with thoroughness, efficiency and success, for within two hours the keep was his. The only disappointment was that Oremund and his crony Raedan escaped, hacking their way through a thin spot in his line. They made a run for the forest that they knew better than him and Brice knew this was not their last stand. Overwhelmed by the strength in his numbers and by the desertion of their lord, Thaxted's men-at-arms surrendered.

By nightfall, the keep had been cleared of bodies and thoroughly searched from top floor to donjon below. Anything of value was secured and all stores would be counted so that Brice could know what he had and what he needed to begin rebuilding Thaxted. The injured were seen to and the dead were blessed and buried. Once the necessary things were done and guards set in a perimeter along the roads leading to and from Thaxted, he allowed himself to think about Gillian.

Reports about her condition had been brought to him throughout the day, so he knew that the arrow had been removed, that she'd lost a considerable amount of blood and that she remained unconscious. And she'd been moved to his tent for privacy and was under the care of one of the camp women. He'd carefully listened and then put the information aside while he concentrated on the battle.

Now, though, he went to find her, and if she could be moved, to take her into the keep where she could be comfortable and cared for. Her room had been prepared, straightened from disarray caused by a search and with a fire laid to warm her.

Ernaut stood at the entrance to the tent, greeting him with his lip curled slightly in a mutinous expression. The boy was not happy about being relegated to the back when the fighting had ensued. His displeasure was something Brice understood, for his squire believed himself ready for battle and wanted the opportunity to achieve the status of manhood that fighting would give him.

'The lady?' he asked as he approached.

'Still asleep, my lord,' Ernaut replied, reaching to lift the flap of the tent.

Brice stepped closer and lowered his voice. 'I would ask that you remain my lady's guard, Ernaut. As you can see, not even her family can be trusted. But I know that you can.' The boy's face beamed with pride then, the recent displeasure replaced now. 'I know you will not fail her.'

'Aye, my lord,' he agreed, standing a little straighter and taller than a moment before.

Brice ducked inside and found Gillian on his pallet, covered by blankets. The woman who'd been caring for her stood and nodded to him.

'She sleeps?' he asked, kneeling to have a closer look.

'Aye, my lord. She has not wakened since she was…'

He leaned over and smoothed the hair from her face, noticing how pale she was. Easing the blankets down, he saw that her gown had been cut away and her shoulder covered in a thick layer of bandages. Blood stained them red, a sign her bleeding had not been completely stanched.

'Can she be moved yet?' he asked. He had little experience in dealing with the injured. He handled the small ones himself when he suffered them in battle, but this was more serious… and she was a woman, not a hardened warrior. 'The winds carry the smell of storms and I would have her more secure within the keep.'

The woman nodded at him. 'As long as the move is smooth, it should not worsen the bleeding. And, as you say, my lord, the storms threaten.' She moved over to Gillian's side. 'Let me prepare her to be moved.'

Brice stood back and allowed the woman more room. He called to Ernaut and ordered his own belongings be gathered and moved to the keep now, too. Once the lady's clothing was back in place, the bandages secured and her cloak wrapped tightly about her to keep her from moving, he knelt at her side opposite the injury and slipped his arms beneath her. Lifting her from the pallet and into his arms, Brice waited for the woman to adjust the cloak and then carried Gillian from the tent.

'Your name, mistress?' he asked the woman who'd tended Gillian.

'I am called Leoma, my lord.' She walked at his side through the crowded camp.

'And your man?' All women here either had a husband or sought one.

'My husband is Danyel,' she replied.

A good man—Brice had known him in Brittany. He'd served under the same commander as Brice himself had and then he'd offered his services to Giles. And Giles had allowed him to serve Brice now.

'Will you come and serve my lady in the keep? She will need help as she recovers.'

'Aye, my lord.'

Brice did not speak again until he entered Gillian's chambers and placed her on the bed there. 'I will see that Danyel knows you are here. Stay with her until I return.'

If he did not consider his actions at that moment, or even later, it was because he was certain he had the correct amount of concern about the woman who was his wife now—no more, no less. He would see to her comfort and her care as was his responsibility. Brice had heard several stories about the lady and imagined what she would be like during his travels here. Nothing had prepared him for the woman herself.

He'd interpreted her running away from Thaxted and her brother as wilful disobedience when that was not the issue. He'd thought her to be an empty-headed, flighty girl who acted impulsively, but he was learning that her actions were usually thought-out and well considered. And worst, he had thought that she felt no responsibility to her people, when she argued for them even when her own life was in danger and under attack.

So, after he returned to the chamber and allowed Leoma to go to her husband, Brice did nothing but think. So many connections as yet unseen. So many dangers to hold at bay. Still so many enemies to battle. Even when his body hungered for sleep, his head was filled with more and more questions. But every question came back to the woman lying unconscious in the bed.

And, when fever struck in the middle of the night, Brice prayed that he would have a chance to know her better, never realising that he worried over her more than he thought he should.

Gillian fought to keep from screaming.

Her brother liked nothing more than to know his punishments hurt and made her afraid, so she'd learned early in his abuse to persevere silently or it brought on more or worse. Now, her jaws ached from clenching them tightly, to keep the sounds of her anguish inside.

Had he lit her aflame? Her skin burned and heat poured through her. She wanted to ask for water, something to soothe

the dryness and flame, but did not dare. Any weakness shown was one used against her later. When the fires grew hotter still, she knew she moaned. Resist as she might, the pain was stronger than her control.

Gillian tried to force her eyes to open, so she could see what punishment he inflicted, but she could not. Then she felt a cooling cloth against her face. And again, it stroked along her cheeks and down on to her neck and the fire receded. Soft whispers joined the coolness and Gillian thought she might survive after all.

Then, as quickly as it came, the soothing ended and the punishment returned anew. At some point, the pain overwhelmed her and she cried out, unable to stop it.

She was so tired of the fear. So tired of the pain and torment. So tired of…everything.

Gillian gave up the struggle and let herself sink away.

The next time she came to awareness, she could hear someone moving about in the darkness near her. The fire was gone, but the pain still pierced her. Now, though, it seemed centred on her left shoulder and arm. Even without the torment of the heat, Gillian could not move—it was as though all of her strength had seeped away, leaving her as helpless as a newborn.

She opened her eyes, finally, and looked around. She lay in her own bed in her own chamber at Thaxted! Had she dreamt the torment and the trials of the last days? Had some illness tricked her mind into believing she'd escaped and been found by the Norman lord she was promised to in marriage? Gillian tried to lift her head, but could not.

'Are you awake now, lady?'

Gillian recognised that deep voice. When he stepped closer, she could see a very different Brice from the others she'd witnessed since meeting him. This one wore a ragged beard, had dark circles under his eyes and looked as though he had not slept in days. She tried to answer, but the words stuck in her dry throat and made her cough.

'Here, now,' he whispered as he slid his hand beneath her head and lifted it higher, 'have a sip of this before you try to speak.'

This was watered ale, which tasted wonderful and felt even better on her parched throat. She swallowed several times and would have drunk more, but he took the cup away from her mouth and she had not the strength to follow it.

'Easy…easy.' His voice held a hint of amusement along with the appealing accent she was coming to enjoy. 'There will be more if you keep this down.'

'What happened? How did I come to be in my own bed?' Gillian glanced around again to make certain she was not in the throes of a dream. 'My brother?'

Lord Brice turned the chair next to her bed around, straddled it and faced her. 'Your brother fled during our attack.' He paused then and stared at her as he answered the other questions she'd posed. 'After he had shot you from behind…after we came in through the tunnel. Once you'd stopped bleeding—well, mostly—I brought you here so you could be more comfortable.'

'How long, my lord? How long have I been unconscious?'

'This is the fourth day since you were injured,' he said, the exhaustion clear in his voice. 'The fever hit late that same night and you have been racked with it for these three days and nights since.' He met her gaze. 'It broke this morn.'

She pushed herself to sit up, but got no further than before. Even the attempt at moving her arm caused bolts of pain to shoot through her injured shoulder and down her arm. She gasped at the strength of the pain and lay back down, trying not to move it again.

'And you have been here since?' she asked.

He shifted on the chair, stretching his arms up and across his chest. He shrugged and shook his head.

'Most of the nights,' he said. 'Leoma has been your more constant companion and caregiver during the days.'

'Leoma?' Gillian asked. That name did not sound familiar to her. Once her old maid died, Oremund had never allowed her to have one who would gain her loyalty. He sent in whichever woman shared his bed at that moment to help her when needed. Leoma was not a name she'd heard before.

'She is married now to one of my men, but she is from Taerford. She tended to your wound and your needs while I saw to my duties.'

He stood then and walked to the small brazier in the corner. Returning with a metal cup, he placed it on the table and then helped her to sit up. It took more effort than he could know to stay upright then, for her body wanted to sink back into the depths of the rope-strung bed and not do such a foolish thing again. When she could finally sit without his help, he brought the cup to her mouth.

'Some beef broth to strengthen you,' he said, tilting the cup. 'Leoma said I should make you drink it if you woke.'

She took several sips from the cup and felt the strong, warm broth fill her belly with its flavour and heat. 'And where have you slept?' she asked.

'Here.' He pointed to the chair.

She knew it for the lie it was as soon as he'd said it—his appearance told her the truth. He'd not slept since she'd been injured. She allowed him to feed her several more times before she waved the rest off with a shake of her head.

'What time of day is it, my lord?'

He walked to the window in the wall and pulled the leather covering. Flashes of lightning filled the chamber now and she could hear a pelting rain falling. Very little light other than the storm entered. 'Just past nightfall,' he said, 'but 'tis difficult to tell with the way the storm has been raging these last three days.'

Gillian was convinced that he would not leave her side, so she ordered him to. 'You must get some rest, my lord, or you will be in no condition to defend your keep when Oremund returns.'

He stared at her, surprised, she could see, by her words. He shook his head. 'He is gone, Gillian. There is no trace of him for miles. My men have searched.'

'Gone for now. He will return when he has men enough to force you from this place. Doubt it not, my lord,' she said. If he did not realise it, it would not be for lack of her trying. ''Tis not in his manner to let go of something he wants.'

Then, as suddenly as she'd awoken, her body began to sink towards sleep. She found it difficult to keep her eyes open or to frame a logical argument with him. And harder still not to reveal the true reason for Oremund's obsession with her.

'Let me help you,' he said before she could ask for it. 'You are not well and will need more time to recover.'

Lord Brice assisted her in sliding down with as little help from her bad arm as possible. If she allowed him to hold it immobile and followed his instructions, her arm and shoulder, indeed her whole body, did not hurt as much. When he would have moved away, she clutched at his hand, not allowing him to.

'Please, my lord,' she whispered, now forcing the words out. 'See to your needs and get some rest,' she urged. Her hand slipped from his and she fell back against the pillows that supported her. 'Please.'

Whether he followed her advice, she knew not, though he was gone when she woke in the night. A candle left burning showed her the chamber was empty, with Ernaut standing next to her open door.

The next thing she knew it was morning and Leoma busied herself with some mending, sitting in the same chair where Brice had sat. The sun's light brightened the room once the leather coverings were tied back and Gillian found herself ready to sit for longer periods and eat and drink more.

A few days later, she could get out of bed with little help and was able to put her syrce and cyrtel on over the bandages. Although her husband always visited her, he never stayed for longer than a few minutes and never spoke on matters of importance. As she'd grown stronger, her mind had filled with many questions for him, but he did not remain long enough for her to ask. Any attempts to get his attention failed. Anytime she tried to leave, both Leoma and Ernaut stopped her.

Worse, no one would give her any details about the battle and the number of deaths. No one would tell her who remained behind when her brother left or who followed him. And no one would tell her what plans Lord Brice was making for defence against her brother's return.

Finally, after a sennight had passed and she felt ready to snap angrily at anyone who entered her room, a sure sign she was well enough to leave it, Gillian took advantage of Leoma's absence to use the other way out of the keep that no one knew about. If no one would speak to her about Thaxted and its people, she would find out for herself.

Chapter Eleven

Gillian discovered quickly that she was not as recovered as she first thought—it took her almost an hour to get down the small staircase cut into the stone wall. With her injured shoulder and arm hanging in a sling, making it down the stairs was difficult at best. Then, when she finally reached the bottom, she needed time to catch her breath before even trying to open the disguised metal door installed to keep the entrance hidden. Peeking out into the blacksmith's hut, she crept out only when she saw it was empty.

Haefen, the smith, was not working there. He was one of few men she felt safe around, for his wife was her aunt and he was too valuable in time of war for Oremund to exile. He was the reason her father cut the secret tunnel from her room to end here—Haefen was big and strong and could protect her and her mother and see them to safety if need be. Though his fire was burning there, she saw no sign of him now.

Oh, dear God! Had Lord Brice's men killed him when they attacked through the tunnel? She stepped out of the shadows and searched for him. He was the only close relative she had, other than Oremund, and she feared that in trying to save lives, she'd cost him his. Gillian walked to the open side of the hut and looked out in the yard to see if he was there.

Although there was no sign of Haefen, the yard was filled with activity. Men carrying large stones to rebuild parts of the wall. Men cutting felled trees into planks, and others clearly following the orders of Lord Brice's men. She saw neither Haefen nor Lord Brice. Walking along the edge of the buildings, she watched as those inside the wall repaired and built anew. None of Thaxted's people seemed threatened or in danger and they worked alongside the Norman and Breton invaders. Their sullen expressions would have earned a thrashing from Oremund's men, but these new conquerors took no notice, or took no action against them.

Gillian managed to make her way unseen to the place where they kept their horses. A large section of the yard had been fenced in and that was where she finally found Haefen working. Crossing to the fence, she called out to him. He looked well and Gillian felt tears burn in her eyes at the joy of finding him alive.

'Girl,' he said, reaching over the fence to pull her into his arms. As he held her and rocked her, she wanted to scream from the pain, but the comfort of his embrace felt too good at this moment.

'Uncle,' she whispered. 'I am glad you are alive. I feared…I feared…you were dead.' But she was not strong enough yet to admit it had been her words that revealed the secret entrance to the keep to their enemies. He released her and she clutched his hand for support.

'Nay—' he shook his head at her concern '—I heard your brother's plans. I saw this lord's army and knew he would take Thaxted.' He leaned back and examined her from head to toe. 'Your brother said you were dead. Told us he was our only protection against these Normans.' Smiling, he shook his head. 'Should've known you were too ornery to die.'

The tears did escape now and she wiped them away with a quick rub of her hand. 'What of the others? How many did Thaxted lose?'

'Not many. Most of those that died were Oremund's soldiers. Oremund killed a few who tried to escape just after you disappeared. Most of the rest are here, somewhere, waiting to see who ends up as lord.'

Gillian nodded, knowing they both understood that this was not over yet. Before she could ask another question, her uncle interrupted. 'Do you trust this Norman?'

'I am not sure,' she said. Thinking about his actions and hers, she realised that in many ways she did. 'Why?'

'Because he's coming this way and looks like he wants to kill you,' her uncle replied as he climbed over the fence and positioned himself in front of her. 'You seem to get that reaction from many people lately.'

His comment reflected the truth. She did seem to irritate many people, but mostly those who tried to control her. She peeked around Haefen, wincing as the sounds of Brice's angry words reached her. He was back to cursing her loudly and it did not bode well for her or her uncle. Gillian did not fear that he would harm her, but she'd not seen him react to those who challenged him yet. Her uncle could really be the one in danger and she tried to move around him before her husband reached them.

It was clear to Brice as spied her from the guard tower that he would have to tie her to the bed, much as his men had tied her in the tent, if he expected her to remain where he had left her. Looking around the yard as he chased her down, he saw no sign of Ernaut or Leoma, the two who were supposed to be with her anytime he could not be. He tore down the steps of the tower and was almost halfway across the yard when he realised what he was doing and slowed his pace. Lucais, whom he'd left in mid-sentence, followed closely behind and they were joined by several others before he reached the place serving as a temporary area for the horses.

Lucais's gruff laugh every time Brice cursed did not ease his anger, especially not when he watched the burly blacksmith take Gillian in his arms. Nor when his wife seemed quite content to be held. By another man. In public. Brice might have drawn his sword then, but he could not remember until it was in his hand before him. The man recognised the danger, for he stepped in front of Gillian as though to protect her.

And, damn his wife, she stepped back in front of the man when she saw Brice's approach and heard his swearing. In spite of barely being able to stand on her own, in spite of her injury that had yet to heal, in spite of the sword that threatened, she stood her ground. He stopped a few paces before her and lowered his sword.

'Do you never stay where you are put, lady?' he asked, not really wanting an answer. When she began to offer one, he glared at her.

Though it pleased him to see her on her feet, looking better than she had since her injury, from the ghost-pale colour of her cheeks and her laboured breathing, she was not strong enough yet to be traipsing around the yard. Alone.

Embracing men.

'Her late father often lamented of the same thing, my lord,' the man answered for her.

'Who are you?' he asked, leaving off what he truly wanted to ask: who are you that you can be so familiar with my wife? He nodded at the man who had still not released his hold on Gillian's waist.

'My lord,' she said. 'This is my uncle, Haefen.'

He narrowed his gaze at the man he knew only as the black-smith of Thaxted. 'I thought you had no family left, lady. Has one suddenly sprung to life, then?' Suspicion flooded him as he could see no resemblance at all between the two. Some other connection, then?

'I married her aunt, my lord. We are not related by blood.'

The man did not offer a direct challenge, for he was only a blacksmith and Brice was an experienced knight and now lord here and the man could never prevail, but he did not bow and scrape as many did before those supposedly noble born.

'What is your business with him, lady, when you should still be abed and recovering?' Now that he saw the link be-tween them, most of the threat was gone. Still, the first person to whom she ran was this man, and it did not sit right with Brice.

'I wanted only to make certain he lived,' she said, her voice weakening and her face growing paler by the moment.

'Return to your chambers and we will discuss this later,' he ordered.

'I cannot, my lord,' she said.

Her words presented not a challenge to his orders, but an ex-planation, one Brice comprehended only a moment before she became ghostly pale and fainted. Only her uncle's grip on her waist kept her from landing face down in the dirt. Sheathing his sword, Brice relieved the man of his burden and lifted her into his arms, having a care for her bound shoulder.

'Speak to me in the keep,' he ordered Haefen as he walked away.

It took only minutes to carry her back to her chambers and see her safe in her bed. Ernaut was startled when he saw them approach, probably believing the lady was within. Then Brice saw the moment that the young man realised he'd failed in his duty. Brice could not excuse it, but he could not punish something he'd missed, as well.

'My lord,' Ernaut began, opening the door for him and waiting until he laid Gillian on the bed there. Brice touched the back of his hand to her cheek. Thank the Almighty, there was no sign of fever returning.

'We will sort this out later, Ernaut. Where is Leoma?'

The very person approached after Brice placed a blanket over Gillian and waved Ernaut out to the corridor. She carried a tray of food, probably the very task that his wife sent her on while planning her escape. Since both were loyal to him, he suspected no subterfuge, but they both needed to understand the wilful and intelligent foe they faced in keeping her safe, even from herself.

'I found her in the yard. Since she did not sprout wings and fly there and since I know Ernaut did not leave his post unattended, there must be another way out hidden in her chambers.'

The two exchanged glances and then nodded to him.

'See to her, Leoma. I do not think she will have the strength to run again—' the irony of the situation was clear to him '—but I do not want her to endanger herself by trying to.'

Suspecting that another or more secret entrances under the

walls or through them existed, Brice and his men had searched the keep room by room for any sign of them. Including her chamber. And found nothing. Walking back down to the main floor, he found the blacksmith waiting for him, guarded by Lucais. Brice motioned him to follow and led him to a table and benches off to one side where he usually met with his commanders.

He ordered some ale to be brought to them and watched as the serving woman dawdled in getting it. He shook his head, tempted to lose his temper at the slovenly behaviour of the servants, both in the keep and out. Any order was met with a stare and an unseemly delay in carrying it out. Glances and gazes were either empty or filled with malice, and there were no attempts to hide either from him or his men. He'd caught several of his men striking out at such displays, but it was not in his nature to do so.

Or it was not before.

Pouring ale into a metal cup and handing it to the blacksmith who remained standing, Brice dismissed Lucais back to his duties and drank some of the ale.

He knew that Oremund had left spies behind, servants loyal to him, in place to report back on any number of things— numbers of fighting men, stores of food and supplies. Much like the resistance that Giles had faced in Taerford, he must find them out and give them reasons to pledge their loyalty to him.

And he would begin his search with Haefen.

'Are you freeman or serf, Haefen?' he asked, motioning for the man to sit.

'I am free, like the miller and the chandler and the brewer.' He declined the invitation to sit.

'How long have you been here in Thaxted?'

'Born and raised here, my lord. Like most of us,' he replied, though Brice could almost hear the pause in the answer. So he asked the obvious question.

'And Lord Oremund? How long has he lived here?' Brice sipped his ale now, never taking his eyes off Gillian's uncle.

'He came here just after their father died at Stamford Bridge in September last.'

'So recent?' he asked. Oremund behaved as though he'd lived here from his birth when they'd parleyed that morning. 'Where did he live before?'

'Lord Eoforwic gave control of one of his larger estates to young Lord Oremund to command a few years ago.'

'Why did Oremund not obey his king's call to arms and fight at Hastings?'

'I do not think I am the right man to answer all these questions, my lord,' Haefen protested.

'But you are a freeman, Haefen. Able to come and go and negotiate your pay and conditions. A much better man to ask than a serf who is completely beholden to his lord and might never know other than his lord's opinion in matters. Indeed, most serfs would not even know of the world outside their gates. A freeman has a wider view of things.'

For a moment, Brice thought this freeman might leave and not answer, but after a drawn-out moment, he did.

'It was agreed that Lord Oremund and Raedan would trail behind and guard the back of King Harold's army.'

This did not make sense, for Duke William received word just before Hastings that Harold had decimated the forces of Tostig and Harald Hardrada. The only forces behind him would have been Mercia's and Northumberland's.

And whose presence at Hastings could have turned the tide against William. Had Harold thought himself in danger from his brothers-by-marriage? Had old rivalries and struggles for power added to the dangers and enemies Harold Godwinson faced in the waning days of his power here in England?

Brice considered that Harold's son Edmund still hid among his followers, and in spite of the fact that his boy-king Edgar the Atheling and the northern earls were in Normandy now with William, there were still enough powerful, disenfranchised Saxon lords and landowners to cause problems. Especially if a strong leader materialised.

He released a deep breath. He'd warned his friend Giles that no good would come from sparing Edmund's life those months ago and now he had a feeling in his gut that the results of that clemency were a pivotal part of what he now faced. Ironic that his fate was still tied to Giles in spite of the miles that separated them.

Thoughts of the woman in her chambers above crept into his mind then. Too many unanswered questions remained.

'What does Oremund want with Gillian?' he asked.

'The same thing any nobleman wants with an unmarried female in his family—to use her to make connections to other families.'

This Haefen knew too much. Brice had the feeling that nothing he could do would make the man betray his niece. Watching the smith cross his arms over his broad chest, Brice wondered which of the two was the teacher and which was the student when it came to stubbornness.

'Is your wife here at Thaxted?'

For the first time since spying Gillian with this man, Brice witnessed a weakness in him. The fleeting glimmer of pain fled quickly and, if he'd not been watching, Brice would have doubted anyone who spoke of it.

'She is dead, my lord,' he replied in a quiet voice that belied the power of the man speaking.

The grander scheme swirled around just out of sight, still vague, but threads of the web began to show themselves to Brice. The one thing clear was that Haefen was still in Thaxted for several reasons, but the first and most important one was to protect Gillian. From him or from Oremund, he did not know yet. Brice finished his ale and stood.

'You may see your niece if you would like. I am certain she has much to talk about with you. Just give her time to sleep and come back before the evening meal.' He waited on the man's reply.

'My thanks,' Haefen said, bowing his head for the first time.

'And on the morrow, bring the other freemen here so that we can discuss the needs of Thaxted and its people. I would have things settled as we rebuild.'

'Aye, my lord.' Another bow. Mayhap some respect growing?

Haefen left; Brice motioned for Lucais to accompany him back to the guard's tower. It was the highest place in Thaxted and gave a view of miles around. And it was the only safe place to talk when he did not wish to be overheard.

It was hours later after his growling belly could no longer be ignored that he finally realised he'd not eaten yet and he'd not spoken to Gillian in any meaningful way for more than a week.

Worse, he'd not touched her or kissed her or even slept in

her bed for fear of worsening her injury. Now, though, after witnessing that she was on the mend, he wanted to see her.

Truthfully, he wanted to peel off every bit of clothing she wore, especially that damned veil that covered her hair and most of her face, and discover what lay under it all while in the comfort of a warm, dry bed, with no one listening and no one near to interrupt. And he wanted to hear those little gasps she made when he touched her most intimate and sensitive places.

Now he was hard again, as always happened when he thought on his wife and he realised he must follow the advice he had given so naively to Giles—begin as you wish to go on. She was his wife before his men who'd witnessed their vows, but to the people here in Thaxted, he knew not what they had been told.

Now that she was recovering, restricting her to her chambers would be seen as making her a prisoner. Surely her uncle's visit would show otherwise, but Brice needed her visible to the people of Thaxted. Though similar to the situation in Taerford, this was different, as well. In Taerford, when Fayth had been out of sight of her people, they began to ask about her and ask for her. Here, not a single person, not even her uncle, had come forwards to show their concern. Not certain of its true meaning, Brice knew only that it was not a good sign.

Those who slept in the main hall of the keep prepared to settle down as he walked through on his way to Gillian's chambers. Brice asked one of the servants to bring some food to him and began to climb the stairs.

Begin as he wanted to go on, he thought. And he knew what he wanted.

Chapter Twelve

Brice noticed that Ernaut remained standing guard in front of her door, straightening as he approached. He would give the boy a new assignment in the morning and begin to rotate other guards through this one. Considering that very few chambers were on this second floor of the keep, someone could stand guard at that stairway and monitor those who came and went. As long as those who had access to the rooms were known to him or trusted by him, Gillian would be safe while in her chambers.

He dismissed Ernaut for the night and opened the door, expecting to find Gillian already abed. Instead, she sat on the chair, wearing only her thin shift and that lay down around her waist as Leoma applied some ointment over the healing wound. Since her back faced him, he could not see her breasts, but it did not matter—his body remembered the look, the feel, the taste and even the weight and fullness of them in his hands. He must have made some sound, for both women looked at him.

This only sent her waist-length hair flowing in enticing waves over her shoulder as she turned only her head to see him. Like some mythical goddess, she stared at him with those blue-green eyes and he lost the ability to speak. The moment drew out until Leoma broke into the silence.

'My lord, we will be finished in a few moments if you'd like to come back,' she said.

Come back? He had no intention of leaving now. He stepped inside and closed the door behind him. 'I can see to my lady's care, Leoma. Why do you not seek out Danyel in the hall below?'

Although it could have become one, the woman quickly realised she would lose if she turned this into a stalemate, for she nodded and held out the small crock to him. 'Apply this to both front and back and cover it with those bandages.'

Brice stepped aside to allow her to leave and then he walked over to Gillian's side. She watched him with wide eyes as he reached out and smoothed her hair out of his path. She clutched the edges of her loosened shift so that her breasts were covered, but it did not relieve the growing desire within him or lessen the beautiful image she presented there. He met her gaze when she gasped at his first touch on the skin near the wound on her back.

'Your pardon, Gillian. I did not mean to hurt you,' he apologised as he softened his touch and began to spread the medicament on the skin farther away from the place the arrow struck.

As she relaxed under his ministrations, he applied it closer and closer, with gentler strokes. Though his mind knew what he did, his body reacted in its own way and soon the blood pounded in his veins and echoed in his head. He wanted her, oh, aye, he did, but this was not the time for such things. Also, he still was not certain that the night spent in her arms before the fight for Thaxted was not simply out of pity on her part. He'd wanted comfort that night; now he just wanted his wife.

Pulling his own needs under control, or making a brave attempt to, he finished smoothing the ointment on the back of her shoulder and moved around her, crouching in front now. Brice had removed his chainmail and other protections before coming here and now discovered that his erection was evident if one looked. He both hoped and dreaded that Gillian would look.

Brice's hand shook then, for now he could see her breasts through the thin layer of linen she held close. He could see her breath catch as she inhaled and noticed that she licked her lips several times as though they were too dry. He tried to ignore it, he tried to ignore the heat growing between them, he even tried not to notice the way her hands began to fall away from shielding her breasts from his sight. The worst, though, was when she closed her eyes and sighed as he touched her.

He dropped the crock and leaned in to kiss her. He would have stopped had she simply looked away or shown any sign of not wanting him to do it, but she turned her face to him and licked her lips one more time. Worse, she opened her mouth as he touched her lips and he lost most of the control he fought to have.

Brice tasted her mouth with his tongue, sliding it in to touch and caress hers. Then, when she imitated the movements with hers, he suckled on it as he wanted to on her breasts and between her legs. He shifted to get closer and let his hand fall to her breasts, allowing the back of his hand to glide over the smooth shift. He felt the tips tighten and he kissed her more deeply, using the other hand to steady her head and hold her close.

He lifted his face from hers and saw her move her hand as though to touch him, and the thrill and anticipation of it caused his erection to surge, larger and harder than before. Trying not to press against her, he waited for that first touch of her hand on him.

The knock on the door seemed so loud and startling that he lost his balance and began to tumble backwards away from her. Regaining his footing at the last moment, he stood and took a step back, noticing the glaze of excitement in her eyes and the blush of anticipation in her cheeks. He remembered telling the serving woman to bring food here only as her voice drifted through the door.

'Your food, my lord.'

Brice watched as the siren became the innocent again, pulling her shift closed and reaching for the shawl that lay over her lap. He helped her gather it around her shoulders, having a care not to jostle the bad one, and then opened the door. Not allowing the woman in, he took the tray from her and closed the door with his foot.

'You have not eaten yet, my lord,' Gillian said. She began to rise from the chair but he stopped her.

'Do not even think about moving from that chair.' He carried the tray over to the bed, placed it there and sat next to it, all without knocking the bowl of soup over and spilling the mug of ale. Considering that his hands still shook, he was quite pleased. 'I have been busy until now.'

'Eat, then.' She nodded to him, rolling her shoulders to loosen them. It was other places in her body that needed to relax, for her breasts ached for more of his touch and that place between her legs throbbed in readiness for more. Feeling this way, with heat building inside her, was new and Gillian was not certain whether it was a good thing or bad.

'Is the pain bad?' he asked in between mouthfuls of the mutton stew the cook had made for their supper. 'Does that hurt?' He nodded at her stretching movements.

''Tis better with each passing day.' Gillian stood then and walked around her chambers slowly, waiting for him to order her otherwise. When he did not, she continued. Standing before him in only her thin shift felt strange, but he'd seen more while he spread the ointment on her skin than he could now with the shawl wrapped tightly around her.

'Did your jaunt out to the yards make it bleed again?'

She stopped and looked at him—he was seeking information about how she'd left the room without being seen. Much as her uncle thought he might be trustworthy, the explanation would not come out of her mouth. She would keep the secret, for now.

'It did not, my lord,' she answered. 'As you may have noticed, the skin is healed over and once the bruising lessens, Leoma says I will have full use of it.'

She did not know how he did not get pains in his stomach from the haste with which he ate, but soon he'd eaten every morsel on the tray and drunk the full mug of ale. When he stood, she expected him to leave as was his custom.

'Am I a prisoner here, my lord?'

She'd wanted to ask the question all day, but feared his answer. Her uncle's arrival had given her hope, but a visitor to her chambers did not mean she could leave. Worse, now that he knew she could get out, would he allow her to stay here or, as he'd threatened during his barrage of angry curses, tie her to the bed to prevent it from happening again?

He let out a breath and shook his head. 'You are not a prisoner, Gillian. Ernaut or another stands at your door for your safety. Leoma is here for your comfort.' He paused and looked at her with a fierce expression, one that made his eyes darken, as he ran his hands through his hair and shook his head.

'At first, when I saw you creeping through the yard, I thought you meant to escape again. You may not think I understand your brother's methods, but I know more about them than you might suspect, and you wandering unattended is simply baiting him into action.' He shook his head. 'Damn it, you are at the centre of whatever he pursues and until I understand why, you will have a guard posted and a companion at your side!'

If she did not know better, she would have mistaken his ire for concern—concern for her—but he was a man used to having his orders obeyed and she had not respected his authority. How would it be to have a husband who truly cared for her and not about the rest of it? He watched her with expectation on his face and so she nodded.

In spite of her claims of understanding him, her brother's actions had been a surprise. Gillian had not appreciated his desperation until he showed his true nature before his enemies. That had not happened before. And a part of her was warmed to have Lord Brice's protection, no matter his reasons. He nodded at her, and seemed calmed a bit by her acquiescence.

'You are not a prisoner, Gillian,' he repeated, but she could not be certain if he was trying to convince her or himself.

Then, he strode over to the far wall, the one where the entrance to the tunnel was and began feeling along the edges. She held her breath, for he was very close to the latch that would spring the door open. Lord Brice slid his hands along the surface for a few minutes and then turned to her.

'Will you tell me where it is?' She started to deny its existence, but he waved her off. 'It is the only way you could have escaped under both your brother's and my watch, so I know it exists. I just don't know where it is.'

'My lord…' she said, trying to think of how to argue the point and failing.

'You do not trust me. I understand.' He turned away as he admitted it to her and Gillian would swear that regret tinged his voice. 'Just tell me how many know its location.'

'Only two now, my lord,' she offered quietly.

His dark eyes narrowed for a moment as he considered her answer. 'You and your uncle,' he said. Before she could deny or admit it, he smiled grimly. 'And I suspect that even your brother could not force the location from Haefen.'

She gasped then, for it seemed he really did know Oremund's ways. Had Haefen told him? Or another?

'Your uncle stays here only to see to your protection, such as he can. That much I know,' he said. 'A debt of honour, I suspect.' Gillian nodded, not trusting herself to say a word.

'But that is not what your brother seeks from you, is it, lady? There is something much more important to him that you control, otherwise he would have killed you the moment he took this keep after your father's death.'

The walls of the room began to twist and spin before her eyes. She tried not to watch them, for it made the dizziness increase. Instead, she reached out, trying to steady herself before she fell. When she could not touch the wall, she clutched the shawl and tried to protect her shoulder from more damage as she pitched forwards.

Instead of the hard wood of the floor or, worse yet, the stone of the wall nearest her, she landed against the hard-muscled chest of Brice. His strong hands held her at the waist and supported her without jarring her injured shoulder. She felt him guide her down and when she regained her wits, she found that they sat side by side on the bed.

He kept his arm securely around her waist, while he gently moved her hair from her face and tugged the shawl free. When he had, he stood with her, pulled the blankets down and helped her onto the bed. His words terrified her, for he spoke of the hours, nay days, spent in the grip of the fever.

'I could not claim to have never killed anyone, but I have never murdered a man. I can be as ruthless in battle as even King William is rumoured to be. It is kill or be killed and a man does what he must to survive, Gillian,' he said as he walked over and blew out the several candles that lit the room. When he reached the last one, he gazed at her over it, which gave his eyes a glowing appearance. 'But I will kill him for what he has done to you,' he promised in a voice so cold she shivered. 'Brother or not, half or full, he will die.'

His breath put out the last candle and she waited for him to leave so that she could think on his fervent promise against her brother. Her head still spun from the fear that she might have revealed something more to him during the madness of the fever, but now her heart warmed from his offer of not only protection but also vengeance against her brother for his acts. Though she occasionally wanted to forgive Oremund for his sins against her and everyone she loved, Gillian knew that not even her father, God rest his soul, would ask that of her.

The fire in the brazier had been banked, so little light was thrown by it, forcing her to listen for his steps to the door.

Instead, his steps came closer to the bed. Then she felt him bump it.

'My lord, the door is in the other direction,' she offered.

'I am not leaving, Gillian.'

She swallowed and sucked in a breath too quickly, making her choke. 'You are not? Where will you sleep then, my lord?'

The ropes supporting her bed protested his weight as he climbed in beside her. He did not move too far onto it as though waiting for her to do so. 'I have decided that I miss the comfort of my wife's arms. I will sleep here.'

She thought to protest or point out her injured shoulder, but the shock of his skin, his naked skin, against her emptied her head of coherent arguments. When had he undressed? And, with a few quick and efficient movements, Gillian found herself stripped of her shift, lying on her good side, with a large, and enlarged, man at her back. She gasped at the sensuous pleasure of being surrounded by his strong muscles, for he slipped one arm under her head and around her body and the other carefully shielded her bad arm.

Her traitorous body reacted immediately, preparing itself for pleasures as it had learned under his touch the last time they'd shared a bed. Her injured shoulder was quickly forgotten as her body softened and opened for him. She did not know how they could accomplish joining without the use of her arm and without a good deal of pain, but her skin and breasts and legs and even inside of her, deep in her belly, ached for him now.

And she waited.

As soon as he settled behind her, he did not move. Oh, that part of him moved, she could feel the heat and strength of it rubbing near the bottom of her back, as though seeking that place between her legs. But he did not press it between their bodies and enter her as he could have. He did not slide his hand to the junction of her thighs and touch the wetness her body, even now, wept at his nearness. And he did not tease and caress her breasts, holding the weight of each in his hand and rubbing the tips until she begged for his mouth there.

The chamber grew silent and, in spite of the heat of his breathing in her ear, he seemed uninterested in the sexual comfort he'd sought the last time. After a few minutes, the warmth and security of his body around hers and the strenuous challenges of the day began to pull her towards sleep. Though convinced she could never fall asleep when such temptation lay so close, her body did eventually succumb. Or it began to until his words prodded her back to wakefulness and anticipation.

'Worry not, Gillian. I plan to seek the comforts of your bed often once your shoulder has healed.'

His voice teased the edge of her ear and he followed it with a kiss on the sensitive skin of her neck, making her shiver. His laughter then, deep and filled with sexual promises, teased her even more, making her want to turn in his embrace and ask him to seek the pleasures of the flesh with her.

'Shhhh…' he soothed then. 'You need your sleep and I need my rest. There will be plenty of time for us,' he whispered.

Gillian felt the exhaustion spreading through her and gave in to it. But the promise of his words and his heat caused the most scandalous of dreams throughout the night. And, in the morning when she woke to an empty bed, she wondered if it had all been a dream.

Chapter Thirteen

'**M**y lady?'

Gillian lay cocooned inside the blankets of her bed alone, though if she let it happen, she could still feel the strength of Brice's arms around her. Ignoring Leoma's voice, she closed her eyes and breathed in the scent he'd left behind.

Masculine.

Leather.

'My lady?' Leoma said again. 'Are you awake?'

Gillian pushed the coverings back and sighed. 'Aye, Leoma, I am awake.'

She was now in spite of her best efforts to remain in that land of sleep and dreams. And, oh, aye, what dreams they'd been! But the brightness that filled her chamber spoke of a delicious spring day outside and it called to her when dreams tempted her back.

'Lord Brice asked if you would join him to break your fast.'

Gillian tried to sit up too quickly and winced at the pain in her shoulder. With some help from Leoma, she managed to slide her legs off the side of the bed and sit up. Balancing was difficult without the use of both her arms. This morn though, the injured shoulder felt better than it had the day before—a good sign for certain.

'Is he waiting now?' she asked, accepting the washing cloth from the woman and wiping her face with it. At Leoma's nod, Gillian smiled. 'Can you help me dress quickly?'

Leoma gifted her with an enigmatic smile, as though she knew something secret, and then assisted Gillian in applying the ointment, placing the bandages and getting dressed. Surprised yet relieved to find her clothing still in her trunk, Gillian selected her favourite cyrtel and veil and soon was on her way down to the hall to greet Brice.

With Ernaut at her side and Leoma trailing behind her, Gillian made her way with care down the stairs, once more feeling less taxed than with her difficult descent yesterday. It was only as she entered the hall that the memories of the last time she'd been here assaulted her and she stopped, certain she would hear Oremund's voice ordering her to Lord Raedan's side.

When she finally looked around the large chamber, she did not recognise it with the changes wrought to it by Brice's arrival. The filthy rushes swept away, the dogs chased and kept out, the tables, benches and floor scrubbed clean—it could have been a different place than Thaxted Keep!

The best part of all was that, for the first time in many, many months, she felt safe as she walked the length of it to reach Lord Brice's side. Gillian did not remember telling him of Oremund's treatment of not only herself, but also their people. However, she'd clearly told him enough that he understood the true nature of her half-brother.

The only thing that marred her return to the hall was the

reaction of the servants who worked both in the hall and kitchen. Though Brice could not see them, they glared at her in open disrespect as she walked towards the Norman and Breton knights near the front of the hall. Some even whispered insults and called her a traitor under their breath as she passed them.

It should not bother her, they were more on Oremund's side than hers, but some of them were brazen enough to make her flinch. Shaken by such hateful words and gestures, she decided to seek her chambers rather than face more insult.

Gillian tugged her hand from Ernaut's grasp and turned, running into Leoma, who was busy flirting with her husband and not watching her step. Despite the pain in her arm from the impact of Leoma's body against hers, she stumbled past and almost ran to the stairway. Without pausing, she climbed the steps and then ran to her chambers. She'd climbed back up on the bed when Leoma tried to enter.

'Go away, Leoma,' she said, loud enough that her words would carry through the door.

'You need to eat, my lady.'

'I am not hungry.' She knew she sounded like a misbehaving child, but the insults had soured her stomach.

'You need to eat, Gillian.'

She closed her eyes against the pull of Brice's voice. Gillian had not seen him as she walked in the hall, for he chose to sit at a lower table and not the one on the dais her brother had constructed for his use, and display. 'Go away. Please.'

'No.'

He did not plead or ask, nor did he order. He simply stated the word with all the inevitability it carried. Gillian slid off the bed and walked to the door, lifting the latch and stepped aside so he could enter. He waved off Leoma's attempts to follow him in and leaned against the door, closing it. She waited for him to do something or say something, but he only watched her.

Then he moved, but it was just his hand reaching for her cheeks and rubbing away tears she did not know she'd been crying. His touch was gentle, and if everything ended tomorrow, she would recall caresses such as these.

'Twice now I have caused you harm, Gillian. Twice when I should have known better or when I ignored words of wisdom from others.'

She glanced down at her arm, thinking he meant that. It ached now from colliding with Leoma, but it was not his fault.

'Not just now, Gillian,' he said softly, his accent more noticeable when he spoke in a low voice. 'Here, sit.' He turned the chair and pointed to it. 'May we speak of important things between us now?'

Just as he waited on her to be ready for seeking pleasure, he'd also waited for her to be ready to face the difficult situations between and around them. But too much time had passed and the dangers grew and he still knew nothing more than he had when he'd taken Thaxted. Looking at the frown that drew her delicate brows into a furrow and the pained expression in her eyes, he realised that even if there was not trust between them, there must be frankness.

'I allowed your brother to dictate the terms and it ended with you being attacked. I thought to learn more of him and his aims and instead learned only more about his viciousness and dishonour.' He paced a few steps away and then back. 'I thought that by removing your brother and demonstrating a

different kind of rule, more like I have heard your father's to
be, I would be accepted by them. Nay, I could gain their trust
and support as I would gain yours.' He raked his hands through
his hair and looked at her. 'Instead, I failed to realise that it
will take more than a fortnight to build something that your
brother demonstrated could be destroyed in a moment.'

Watching her expression change as she'd walked through
the hall just now and seeing the pain, he'd realised the servants were whispering insults to her. Some of them had not
been subtle; his men overheard too many of them. And all of
them indicated seeds of malice sown by Oremund. To get to
the truth, he needed Gillian to explain more about her family
ties and the stakes involved, for there was no one else more
deeply in the middle of it all than her. He crouched down in
front of her, meeting her face to face.

'But to do that and to establish my rule here, I need your
help, Gillian. Will you tell me the truth about your father and
mother and Oremund's claim to Thaxted?'

He watched as a series of emotions crossed her face in only
a few moments, but then she nodded. He moved away then to
give her space and so that he could concentrate on her words
instead of her scent or the way her skin invited his touch.
His body had understood what had happened between them
and the message hers had given as he felt her soften and lean
against him last night. It had been the most difficult exercise
in self-control he'd ever faced. Her willingness and her nearness drove him nearly insane with the need to claim her. And
as a man who never denied himself a willing woman in his
bed, this last sennight had been torture, plain and simple.

'My father took my mother as his leman two years after
Oremund was born. I do not know what happened between

my father and his wife, but 'twas said he never shared her bed again after Oremund's birth. When I was born, things became very difficult between Father and his wife, so he began to spend more time here in Thaxted. Lady Claennis was sent off to one of Father's northern properties along with Oremund. The day after Father received news of her death, he married my mother.'

Brice could think of one good reason for such a visible and public separation, but hesitated to voice it without any other proof than his own suspicions. 'And he continued to live here and Oremund in the north?' Close to both Mercia and Northumbria and the constant mischief of Edwin and Morcar, sons of Aelfgar.

'Aye, and the hard feelings grew. When he came of age, my brother questioned everything my father did, even arguing with him about who were allies and who were enemies. When King Edward died and Harold was declared king, matters got even worse, for when the call came from the king, Oremund refused it. My father had to fight, instead.'

The strands of the web became clearer just then and the growing connections between Oremund and the northern earls spoke of a larger conspiracy than he'd first thought. Had King William thought that by taking Morcar, Edwin and Edgar out of England he would stop their plans? And with Edmund Haroldson still alive and drawing more and more rebels to his ghost army, things could take a bad turn even yet. And his own arse hung out in the open as he tried to gain control over one of the hotbeds of sedition.

He nodded at Gillian. 'And your mother?'

She sighed then and sadness crept into her voice. 'She became ill at the worst of it between my father and Oremund, almost as though she thought she was the cause of their dispute. When she grew ill, my father took her to the good sisters at the convent who were known for their healing skills.'

Brice felt a chill race down his spine and waited for more from her. 'And?'

'She passed away without ever returning to Thaxted. One day, my father received word of her death and by the time we arrived, they had buried her. Since he had given her Thaxted as her dower property, he then named me heiress to it, with Oremund receiving every other property and title on my father's death.'

That niggling chill returned, promising and threatening that there was more, so much more to this, and to Oremund's obsession with keeping Gillian close despite hating her. Before he could ask his next question, the sound of her stomach rumbling broke into the quiet.

She blushed then as he realised that she'd come to the hall to break her fast and had not yet eaten. He held out his hand to her.

'My apologies, lady, for having allowed you to go hungry. Come, food awaits us in the hall below.'

Clearly, she was torn between accepting his hand to return to the place where she'd been unwelcome and staying here in relative safety. Isolated, but safer and less painful.

'Join me,' he said, making it a request rather than an order. This time she took his hand and stood.

As he walked to the hall, he knew what he must do. He'd disdained it when Giles had done something similar, but now understood the need for a public display. Brice guided Gillian down the steps, tempted several times to carry her down, and then inside the hall. Once they arrived there he found that his men, at least, had carried out his orders.

All the servants assigned to work inside the keep stood gathered there waiting for his return. He did not need to make a large demonstration; a small one could be effective and spread the word. When Gillian tried to disappear from his side, he held on to her hand and waited as Ansel called out his name and title.

'Lord Eoforwic, God rest his soul, married Aeldra of Thaxted in the Danish manner and named Thaxted as her mor- gengabe,' he began, filling in a few details he'd learned from others. 'He decreed in his will that Gillian, Lady of Thaxted, was her mother's heiress and would own Thaxted Keep and lands on his death and have no claim on his other estates or titles.'

Holding their entwined hands high enough to be seen by all, he continued.

'By rights of kingship, William of Normandy has named me, Brice Fitzwilliam, Baron of Thaxted, and given me the Lady Gillian in marriage. By the rites of the Catholic Church and before witnesses, she is now my legal wife, confirming her place here…' He paused then, meeting the bold gazes of a few of them. 'Disrespect shown to her is shown to me. Disobedience to her words is disobedience to mine. Discord sown against her will be against me.'

He let her hand go and took a step forwards then, giving a clear message to those assembled and the freemen who'd just entered as well and heard him.

'The punishment is a simple one—I will put you out.'

They gasped then, for the only thing that protected them from the outlaws and villains and criminals was their lord.

The only one who supported them and provided for them was their lord. For a serf attached to the land, being turned out was tantamount to a death sentence.

'Though he is gone from here, those of you who work for Oremund's aim and purposes be warned—I will show no mercy to traitors who follow his real cause. I am William of Normandy, now King of England's man and will uphold his reign and rule.'

Brice stepped back to Gillian's side and finished.

'There is much hard work ahead here and much success to be had, if there is no discord, disobedience or disloyalty. I do not look for trouble, but I will not turn away from it. Now go about your duties and remember my words.'

He watched as the servants moved away and as the freemen approached. But Brice wanted to know Gillian's reaction and turned to face her.

'They fear his return, my lord,' she said softly. 'He made it clear he will do so and hold each of them accountable, much as you have.'

'He will not regain Thaxted, or you, lady,' he said. 'No matter what he has told them or what he plans. It, and you, are mine and I will not give either up.'

He lifted her hand to his mouth and kissed it. A faint pink blush began to fill her cheeks and she nodded, accepting his words. The noises emanating from her stomach ruined the poignant moment and reminded him of his atrocious lack of manners. Leading her to the table where he'd eaten, he called out for food to be brought for her. This time the servants followed his orders quickly.

Lucais had said that he needed to make his place and hers clear to everyone, and this seemed the easiest way to do that.

Brice was not fool enough to think this would turn their loyalty to him, but he had to intervene in some way or Gillian would never be able to live safely in her own home.

When the freemen, including her uncle, approached, he motioned for them to join him at the table and began to negotiate their terms for service in his demesne. Though Gillian said nothing, he only had to watch her face and eyes to see if he was offering too much or not enough. Following her subtle guidance, he concluded his talks most favourable for his purse and his people. He dismissed them with the same warning, though a different, more suitable punishment in place if they betrayed him to Oremund.

Though time would tell, Brice wondered how he could make his wife trust him enough to tell him the rest of the truth. And would it be in time to save them all?

Gillian tried not to smile as she observed Lord Brice bargain with the miller, the brewer, the chandler, her uncle and a few other freemen who'd worked for her father. Though her brother had taken over and set his own wages to pay them, a pittance of their true value, this new lord seemed to enjoy the back and forth of offer and counter-offer. He even lapsed into cursing, good-heartedly it seemed, when he did it.

When her uncle had asked her to visit him later, she looked to her husband first. Although he'd said she was no prisoner, saying it and allowing her freedom were different matters. When he offered only a warning not to try to do too much on her first day out of bed, with his eyes darkening at the mention of 'bed', she felt a different kind of warmth spread through her.

The day passed quickly for her, but there was a certain

melancholy thwarting her attempts at being glad of her freedom, and her husband's best efforts to see them all safe from
Oremund's plans. When Brice sent word that he would not be
there for supper, she decided to eat in her chambers. Though
she climbed into bed before he arrived, her body pulsed with
a sense of anticipation over the possibility of pleasure. She'd
felt it when he kissed her hand and gazed at her and it continued to build in her blood and body the rest of the day.

But the comfort of the bed beneath her and her exertions
throughout the day challenged her efforts to stay awake and
wait for him. Soon, her eyes closed on their own and she sank
into sleep.

Lucais had been pleased with the results of his declaration
to the servants in the hall for it meant hot food, faster and more
of it at meals. Stephen was not so certain of the success of the
message and warned that some would disappear from the keep
over the next few days as they returned to, or attempted to find,
their true master. That warning also included a reminder—
Brice was within his rights to capture and kill any escaping
serf who was bonded to this land.

Brice listened to one after the other, having sought their
counsel about all manner of things. Despite the absence of his
closest friends, he found that Lucais and Stephen resembled
them in many ways. Lucais saw the subtleties while Stephen
saw the direct and visible. Both had good minds for planning
strategies and were quick-witted and intelligent.

And loyal without question.

So, Brice decided that Lucais would be his castellan, even
before his stone keep replaced the current wood-and-stone
one, while Stephen would serve as commander of Brice's

fighting men. Ansel would serve Lucais while Richier would be Stephen's second in command. The one thing missing from his organised structure of duty and responsibility was someone in charge of his household.

With everything that had happened to her, Brice thought to wait and let her settle in as wife before making her take on the duties of the household, but as building went on and the demands of planting fields and preparing both crops and livestock for the growing season increased, he needed her help.

As he watched her making her way to the smithy from his now-favourite spot in the guard tower, he wondered if he could trust her.

Chapter Fourteen

Brice was thinking of several different ways to bring up the subject of her duties now as lady of Thaxted as he dismissed the guard and entered her chambers. So when he closed the door and turned to find her sleeping, he was surprised and disappointed. He stood by the bed and considered his next action.

Was he to take it as a sign of willingness that she did not wear anything but her shift? Or was that a sign she meant only to sleep? Was the way she touched her hand to the empty place on the bed an invitation or did it mean she was blocking his entrance?

Being a married man was much more difficult than a bachelor who never had any doubt about the meaning of a woman in his bed, or her presence in his bedchamber.

She shifted then, tossing her head and moving under the covers in the throes of some dream. Not the terrors that plagued her during the fever, though, and he let out his breath in relief that she did not suffer now. Indeed, she smiled in her sleep; her breathing changed to something different from restful sleep, as though she physically exerted herself in her dreams.

Merde.

She dreamt of their joining.

She dreamt of the pleasure they'd share that night.

She dreamt of him, for she whispered his name and it echoed through the silence of the chamber.

And the sound of it pierced his heart and inflamed his body in but a single moment.

His breathing became ragged as his body filled with wanting for her. He hardened and pulsed against the braies he wore. His skin burned from within and hungered for her soft, soothing touch.

He wanted her, wanted her under him, wanted to fill her and take her and mark her as his own. Never once in all of his experiences with women of all sorts had he felt this way about one. Never did he expect the woman he'd claimed as wife to fill him with such expectation and anticipation. Never had he allowed himself to dream of such things.

Until Gillian of Thaxted walked down the road into his camp, telling him a ridiculous story and trying to make him believe it. Until she moaned that hot, sexual sound in the back of her throat when he'd brought her to pleasure.

Until she met his gaze and returned his own feelings of desire for her with an expression of inexperience and wanting that left his mouth dry, his body harder and gave him the permission he needed to enter her bed.

'Gillian,' he whispered, his voice cracking from the need to touch her. He sat on the bed and pulled off his tunic, loosened his belt and braies and tugged off his leggings and boots in a few moments. She reached for the edge of the bed coverings and brushed his thighs as she did so, causing him to shudder in excitement.

Should he put out the candles so that his body, his erection, was not so evident? Gillian licked her lips and he forgot all his questions. For the first time since reaching manhood, he could not seem to do what usually came without much thought—seducing and pleasing women. Now, with so much of his future and hers at stake, he'd lost his way.

'Gillian,' he said once more after clearing his throat. 'I...I... *Merde!*' Then he cursed his own stupidity in the language of his lands in Breton.

'My lord,' she interrupted in a soft voice, 'I have had a long and busy day.' He thought she now meant to refuse him, but the siren was back, and any sign of the innocent vanished. 'I would like to seek some comfort in my husband's arms.'

He nearly exploded in that moment. He throbbed with need and his body screamed at him to move, but all he could do was stare at the woman now his wife. Despite a rather lacking initial joining, apparently she was more than willing after he'd shown her how good it could be between them.

Brice pulled the covers back, but instead of lying next to her he climbed on to the bed and sat against the headboard and wall. Gently, and with great care for her arm, he lifted her by the waist and guided her to sit on his lap. He intended to ease her shift off, and then decided quicker action was needed. The satisfying tearing sound of the fabric as he pulled it apart was only surpassed by the view of her ample breasts it gave him. Tossing the shift aside, he moved her closer so that she straddled him.

He did not know if she gasped or he did at the intimate touch of that place between her legs and his shaft, but the pleasure nearly overwhelmed his meagre control. This position both opened her woman's flesh to his touch and brought her breasts, now blushing an enticing shade of pink as their tips pebbled, to within kissing distance of his mouth. She closed her eyes then and he touched the place that had haunted his dreams.

She was hot and wet and his fingers slid over the slick folds and found that deeper channel where he ached to be. To make certain she did not fall, he lifted her good arm up to brace against his chest and then he caressed her until she moved against him. First with one finger, then two, then with the fingers of one hand and then with the fingers of both hands, moving faster and harder against the swelling folds and seeking that bud between them.

Gillian dropped her head back and let out the moan she'd been holding inside. He touched her and rubbed her until she felt on fire. She tried to move against him, tried not to fall on to him, tried not to surrender to the passion growing within her, but she gave up all struggles and fell into the pleasure with him.

He teased her without mercy and each time she approached that pinnacle of feeling, he slowed his movements and they became soothing instead of inciting her. She managed to lean up on her legs and move along him, but he stopped her with his hands on her waist. When she protested, he laughed and took the tip of one of her breasts in his mouth and suckled on it. Just as she could feel the release building again, he stopped.

She begged then, for release, for pleasure, for more, for anything, but he would not quicken his pace. When his mouth closed over the other nipple, she reached down and touched him. The growl should not have surprised her; she knew that part of him was sensitive, extremely so, but it served him right for denying her. Without warning, he lifted her hips, placed his hardness directly under her and then allowed her to slide down, inch by excruciating, enticing, exciting inch until he was planted completely within her.

How he could fit inside her, she knew not, for from the size of him she could not believe it. Her body became a thing of its own then, shifting so that she could move along his length. His grip on her hips prevented her, but when he suckled on her other breast and touched that spot between her legs with his other hand, she nearly fainted from the sheer pleasure. She felt her inner walls tighten around his hardness, forcing her body ever closer to that promised peak.

Finally, she begged him once more for release and he smiled that wicked smile she saw only during their joinings and nodded his head. But if she thought he would bring her to pleasure quickly, she was wrong again. Each time they did this, he followed a different path. Each time he paced it so that she never knew what to expect and she tumbled madly through it as he led her body with his caresses and kisses and more.

Now she could feel the signs that her body was ready for that last step. The heat pulsed through her, her blood pounded through her veins, her womb throbbed in anticipation. So when he took her by the waist and gently tumbled her back on to the bed, interrupting the pleasure, she cried out.

'Ah, Gillian,' he whispered as he moved her body on the bed, not allowing her to expend any effort at all. 'Now I will show you what I dreamed of doing…what I promised to do once we shared a bed.'

Soon her legs were hanging over the side, exposing her tender, excited flesh to both the chill of the room and to his sight. When she tried to cover herself there, he laughed and her body reacted to the deep, throaty tone of it. But instead of moving her hand, he guided one of her fingers deeper between to touch…herself! She raised her head to watch him kneel between her legs and could not imagine his purpose.

'Show me where you want me to touch you, Gillian,' he ordered. 'Use your finger and show me.'

She never expected that she could gain pleasure from her own touch, but she did as she slid her finger there, searching for the places he'd touched before. He opened her legs wider and laid them over his shoulder for support. She touched the first spot where it ached the most and then shuddered when he licked it.

'My lord,' she said, trying to move away from the incredible feelings such a touch caused, but he held her hips so she could not.

'You promised to call me Brice,' he said as he dipped his head nearer once more. 'Show me another place, Gillian.'

Her body arched this time when his mouth followed her finger and he suckled the aroused flesh there. But she did as he ordered, touching herself and then trembling and shuddering as he licked and tasted and suckled his way across and over that forbidden place. Then her hips arched forwards and every muscle in her stomach and belly and even her womb tightened and tightened until she could take no more.

Just as the first wave of pleasure poured through her, he moved to stand and filled her with his hardness in one, deep, continuous stroke. The force of it pushed her back away from the edge and he followed her body, thrusting again and again and again until she could not breathe. He climbed with her, continuing to push his rock-hard manhood deeper and deeper until she cried out from the ecstasy of being possessed so completely.

Gasping and gasping, she watched as though from outside

herself as her body accepted his and as he began to spill his seed within her. He clenched his jaws and looked in pain, but she knew he was not. Not any more than she was, but as she reached that peak of stimulation and her body spilled its wetness, she enjoyed the way she could feel her inner muscles clutch his hardness and not let it go.

Minutes passed, or hours, she knew not, until their bodies relaxed from the intensity of the excitement, but she could feel him still large and hard within her. And any movement, any movement, sent tremors through her. He did not, she noticed, fall against her; instead, he kept most of his weight off of her.

'You used your mouth there,' she said, still stunned by such an intimacy as she felt him throb inside of her. Gasping again, for the sensation was pleasure bordering on pain, he eased himself out from between her legs. 'Your mouth.'

Gillian knew she must seem so naive when he compared her to the others before her, but she never knew such a thing was possible or could bring so much pleasure. He lay at her side now, his hand on her belly, the weight of it somehow soothing after such arousal.

'There are many ways to find pleasure, *chérie*. And when your arm is completely healed, I will take no mercy on you as we find it together,' he promised wickedly. Her body trembled at such thoughts as the ones that sped through her mind in that moment. Could she truly even imagine what he meant by that?

He slid from the bed and offered his hand to help her sit. The coverings were a mess, her torn shift lay on the floor and the candles were still burning. Her breasts and between her legs felt heavy and aching from his attentions and she doubted she would sleep now. She watched the way his strong muscles moved as he walked over to the table and brought back a cup of ale for her to drink. But when he leaned closer, he touched his mouth to hers in a gentle kiss.

She could taste herself on his lips. It was shocking, as shocking as touching herself had been, but it excited her in much the same way. Gillian licked her lips then, noticing the salty taste of her body's wetness.

'If you continue to do that, you will find me between your legs again, lady,' he said, staring at her mouth once more.

For a moment, the silence spun out between them and she was not certain what would happen. Her body readied for him, that place already throbbing in anticipation of his lips and tongue. Then he shook his head and poured himself some ale, mumbling under his breath something she could not understand. When she bent over to retrieve her shift from the floor, he shook his head and the smile and words he offered were not genuine at all.

'Your pardon, Gillian, for destroying your shift. I did not mean to do so,' he said.

He meant not a word of it and she laughed, accepting it as the false apology it was. He grabbed the balled-up garment and tossed it on the trunk where she kept her clothing. 'You need not wear anything when we share a bed, lady. I fear I cannot vouch for the safety of such garments if you choose to.'

Brice wanted her naked when he held her in his arms, without even a thin piece of linen in his way. Even now, his body reacted and it would not take much to bring it to hardness again. One look, one lick of her tongue over her lips, one movement against his flesh, and he would be ready to take her.

How did she do it? No other woman incited him to such

madness as she did. The thought of spending the rest of his life in her bed, in her arms, deep in her body, did not frighten him the way he thought it would. Indeed, he could even imagine seeking only her bed if this was the fervent welcome he would receive. He shook his head then in wonderment at such a thought as he blew out the candles and walked to the bed.

Having the same woman as wife and lover was not something he'd thought could be done. Kings—well, kings had an entire collection of lemans, concubines and a legal wife or two, though the Church sought to control all such marriages now. Noblemen had lemans for their physical needs and wives to bear their heirs. Even peasants did not always marry—the lack of a priest to bless them made it more likely that they would simply live together and have children together.

He pondered this new appeal of the lovely Gillian as he assisted her into the bed and drew the covers up over them. Easing her into the same position as last night, he realised two things—he was not tired yet and he was hard and ready again. He would have fought off the urge to take her again, but she shifted her shapely bottom against his flesh and softened for him.

As he slipped between her now wet folds and filled her from behind, this time at her urging, Brice also remembered the issue he needed to discuss with her. But he was soon lost in the haze of desire as their bodies sought and found more pleasure than he'd ever expected with his wife.

So much for his plan to postpone taking his wife to bed until her injury healed completely. He was like some unleashed, ravening beast, filled with mindless hunger for her. If she looked at him as he walked through the hall or keep, he would find her, take her to her chambers and make love with her until they could not move. If she spoke to him and her voice took on that sexual tone or she said a word that reminded him of the way she would beg for his touch, they ended up in bed. And heaven forbid she should touch him, for no matter how innocently it happened, it led to hours of pleasure.

Once they barely made it to the privacy of her chambers clothed. Another scandalous time, they were in the stables when he tossed up her skirts and took her against the fence as a stallion took a mare in heat.

It was scandalous, it might be undignified, it was shocking and Brice loved every moment of it. He kept waiting for Gillian to give some sign that she tired of his attentions, but it never happened. He convinced himself that he would abide by her request when it came and he would not seek her bed, but each night or day she smiled at him and opened her arms to him and her body to his and he prayed that she would never tire of him.

She'd taken to lovemaking like a...

'A pig in shit,' Lucais said.

Startled, Brice looked at him and then around him for such a creature. Then he realised he'd been dreaming of her again, awake, in the middle of the day. All because he spied her walking through the yard on some errand or another and lapsed into lustful thoughts. Again.

Lucais smacked him on his shoulder and laughed. 'I said that you and the lady have taken to marriage like a pig in shit,' he explained. 'Women all over Brittany and Normandy are lamenting over the loss of two of their beautiful bastards.'

'Just so,' Brice answered, shaking himself from his reverie. 'When Simon married Elise, I knew it was the end of the world as we knew it!' he said, laughing. They'd always tried not to take their reputations too seriously, for it was more about fool-ish pursuits than serious ones. Of course there was a third one lost, as well, but at least he was alive.

'We were discussing…?' Brice had truly lost track of their conversation, though he loathed admitting it even to Luc, who shook his head and laughed once more.

'How many acres of wheat we should plant this season,' his castellan reminded him. 'And barley.'

Brice knew little about agriculture, having focused on his fighting skills, expecting to live out a life as a mercenary, fighting for whichever lord could pay his fee. Now, though, it was his responsibility, for the fruitfulness of the crops led to the success of his position here in England. Not as exciting as a battle, but it could be much more lucrative.

But more than that, it was about putting down roots, build-ing a family, a place of his own. For that, he would learn about crops and fields lying fallow and how many goats and cows and pigs they needed to sustain themselves. Luckily, men like Lucais, who came from a large estate in Anjou where his father was steward, never lost their knowledge when they picked up the skills of a knight and were a great help.

Giles had the benefit of keeping mostly all the villeins and freemen who'd lived on Taerford before he gained its lands, but Oremund had successfully chased off, killed or moved most of the original people of this estate, thus leaving Brice the task of rebuilding not only the land, but also the people.

Lucais pointed out several fields from their vantage point and discussed his plans for them, but Brice's attention had al-ready been drawn to his wife's lush figure as she walked across the yard towards the keep. Though she chatted with Leoma and another woman and was the perfect picture of innocence, he knew the woman beneath the facade now. The one who shed her inhibitions as he shed her clothes. The one who gave herself to him in breathtaking abandon. And, unfortunately, the one who trusted him completely with her body, but not yet with her secrets.

Brice realised he must regain his control and find out the reasons behind Oremund's obsession with this place and with her. And it had to be soon, for his spies had returned with reports of Edmund Haroldson being seen in the area. That could be no good. He let out his breath and shook his head, still watching the sway of Gillian's hips as she walked.

He'd spent a fortnight joyously swiving his wife while danger escalated around him. Finding Edmund and Oremund was a necessary task and one that needed to be done immediately. No more dallying with his wife. No more waiting and watching.

It was time.

Chapter Fifteen

Gillian sat at the table alone.

Well, the dozens of others who ate around her belied that claim, but without Brice there, it seemed empty. Looking around, she noticed that more than a few of his men were also missing from supper.

Their lives had settled into a pattern over the last fortnight. He'd asked her to take over the duties of overseeing his, their, household and she'd accepted. She doubted he knew the significance of his request, but she did, as did those of Oremund's people who remained here. Brice had carried through on his words that she was lady here, in name and in fact, and that he trusted her.

Duties that her mother had trained her to take on were now hers. Duties her father had given and her brother had taken were hers once more.

Duties that included seeing to his meals.

He'd sent no word that he would not be here, indeed, he'd walked past her in the yard, acknowledging her with a silent nod of his head before mounting his horse and riding out of the gates with a small troop of his men on some task. She'd turned and watched and waited for some private sign or expression as had become their custom these last few weeks, but he gave none. He never even turned to look at her as he rode off.

She finished her meal, though it turned tasteless in her mouth as she thought of Brice's behaviour. After giving orders to keep enough warm for those who'd missed the meal, she climbed the steps to her room to wait for his return.

Mayhap it was the beginning of her courses that made her feel so different? Could he tell they'd begun? Had someone told him and so he had no desire for her now? Is that how it was between husbands and wives?

She had no memory about her parents' marriage, or their pursuit of passion together, something she did not want to dwell upon. And though her own marriage was often discussed, she'd not had any idea of what truly happened in the marriage bed until she wed. Oh, she'd seen and heard things and even heard bawdy comments from men and women about the physical aspects, but until Brice had done some of those things to her and with her, she never understood them.

Now, she understood. And she wanted him.

She reached her chambers and looked for the mending that needed to be done. Sitting nearest the table where several candles burned, Gillian began stitching the torn fabric, replacing missing buttons and making other repairs.

Was it a bad thing to want him so much?

She certainly had not felt this way about Lord Raedan, Oremund's crony and the one he'd promised her to. Raedan was old enough to be her father, older still than that, and his wrinkled skin hung in folds around his neck. His breath stank and his touch was worse still. She shuddered just thinking of what would have awaited her in his bed and could not imagine such intimacies with him as she'd shared with Brice.

Now that she thought about it, Oremund had never promised marriage to him, only that she would be Raedan's. Brice's missive, telling of King William's granting of Thaxted to him, only hurried Oremund's efforts along. He could not turn her over to Raedan until he found out where the missing fortune was and he could not abandon Thaxted without her. Her frequent escapes or attempts slowed him down and then, thankfully, Brice's arrival with his troops stopped it.

Gillian closed her eyes and offered up a prayer of thanksgiving for deliverance from her brother's plans. Despite Brice being a foreigner, an invader, the supporter of an enemy king, he was the best thing that could have happened to Thaxted and to her. She only hoped that his change in behaviour this day was not a sign that he now thought their marriage a mistake.

'Do you pray for his soul or mine, dear sister?'

A voice she heard in her nightmares floated from the shadows of the room. With the light of the candles so close to her, it was difficult to see into the corner of the chamber.

Near the door to the tunnel.

Oremund stepped forwards, bringing himself into the circle of light, and bowed to her. 'Or for your own, to pray God to forgive you for your disobedience?'

Gillian glanced at the door, wondering if she should call out for help. Before she could, he drew his short sword and blocked her. 'How did you find it?' she asked. Only she and her uncle knew of the tunnel.

He laughed quietly, but no less dangerous for the lack of volume. 'Did you really think I did not know how you escaped from your chambers? One of your loyal servants sold that information to me. Loyalty is much overrated, you know.'

Her uncle would never have revealed it to him. Never. So, she'd been betrayed by someone else in the keep, then.

'It worked nicely to let everyone believe that you were a witch like your mother before you,' he snarled.

'I am no witch, Oremund, and you know that.'

'Ah, but you whore as well as your mother did. I can even smell him on you now.' He sniffed in a vulgar manner at her. 'And you swive him like the whore you are.'

She moved so quickly, it surprised even her, crossing to him in a few steps and reaching up to slap him for such an insult. But he was faster and stronger, blocking her blow and grabbing her hand. She tried to pull free, but could not.

'He is my husband,' she argued.

'A bastard who will soon be buried with those who have tried to stop my plans, sweet Gillian. And I suspect that Lord Raedan will be grateful for the bedplay the bastard has taught you. He has a wider range of tastes for pleasure of the flesh than most and you will likely be more appealing now that you've been broken in for him.' She gasped and tried to pull away again. 'Virgins can be so tiresome.'

He released her this time when she tugged and she stumbled across the room. 'What do you want, Oremund?'

'The same thing I have wanted from you since your whore mother stole it—the gold that should be mine.'

Gillian rubbed at her wrist and shook her head. 'It was part of her gift from our father on their marriage.' She backed away when he lifted his hand. 'I know you refuse to believe it, but they said vows and she was his wife when she died.'

He came closer, grabbed her tunic and pulled her to face him then, rage filling his face and pouring from his mouth.

'That whore stole my father from his rightful, legal wife and stole my inheritance from me. Now, if you value your life and that of the Breton you've crawled into bed with, you will tell me where it is.'

If she'd learned only one thing in dealing with her half-brother it was never to try to argue with him when rage controlled him. It led to nothing good and she'd most likely said too much already.

'Do you not think I would tell you if I knew?' she asked quietly. 'When you beat me or kept me without food or water? When you killed my servants in front of me? When you forced my uncle to watch as you killed my aunt to try to make him reveal it to you? If I knew, Oremund, I would have saved them from their fates. If there is gold, 'tis not worth the price I have paid for it.'

Oremund took a step back and released his grasp on her. 'Tell me where it is, Gillian, and I will never come back to this piss-hole you seem to like so much.' He took in a deep, rasping breath and let it out. 'Tell me and you can keep that Breton in your bed.' He paused and stared at her. 'Tell me.'

She was about to deny knowing its location when a commotion began out in the yard. From the orders being called out, it would seem that her husband had arrived.

'You have your inheritance, Oremund. Our father left you everything—his titles, his estates in the north, his belongings. Everything is yours.' She shook her head then. 'There is no fortune—if there ever was one. Father said he gave it into my mother's keeping to safeguard it, for a time of need. He never spoke of it after her death and never revealed its whereabouts to me.'

'It exists, Gillian. It exists and it's mine. I will find it.'

'I think if it did exist, Father may have used it to pay for the costs of going to war,' she offered him the same excuse she'd told herself many times.

As the sounds of men entering the keep grew louder, Oremund glanced at the door to the corridor, the door to the secret passage and then at her, as though gauging the time needed to escape.

'He would not leave his whore nor his bastard daughter a penniless bitch with only this pigsty as her holding unless there was gold to support it—we both know it. Find the gold and return it to me or more will suffer for your stupidity and wilfulness.'

Without delay, he stepped to the wall, tripped the latch and disappeared into the darkness of the hidden stairway. Just as it closed, Gillian heard Brice's approach in the hallway.

How could she keep him from knowing? Should she? Staring at the wall that hid the tunnel, she realised that Oremund or his men could be coming and going whenever they wanted. How they got inside the walls she knew not, but she would not put it past him to have dug his own secret entrances if he knew of their father's.

Gillian took several deep breaths, trying to release the tension and fear in her body so that she could greet her husband calmly. She'd told Oremund the truth about the gold—though her father had promised it, she'd never seen it. If her mother had hidden it, the secret had died with her, for Father never mentioned it after her death. And now, if it could be found, it belonged, by law, to her husband.

If it could be found.

The soft knock warned her of his entrance and she turned to face him.

Brice had had a miserable day, ever since realising that his infatuation with his wife was getting in the way of carrying out his duties effectively. He'd done nothing but think about her, as he worked in the keep, in the yard and then when he left to accompany Stephen and some of the men on a search of the forest.

That had been the worst moment. He could see the expectation of something more in her eyes and he had passed her by without a word. Others called out to her as they rode out, but he did not, fearing his resolve would crumble. And it had; almost as quickly as he'd decided his course with her, he changed it back.

Then later, sitting in the rain as they planned their search of acres of forest and positioning of guards on the roads to report on any movement of numbers of men, he decided to keep to his new course.

Now, as he tried to walk up the steps and not rush to her chambers, as he tried to control his need for her, it seemed like a mistake. He opened the door after knocking.

Something was wrong, terribly wrong. He could see it in her eyes, in the paleness of her face, in the way she stood. He closed the door first and walked over to her slowly.

'Are you well, Gillian?' he asked, trying to assess her condition. Mayhap some sickness afflicted her? He reached up to touch her cheek and she flinched.

Something was terribly wrong.

'Are you well?' he asked again when she did not answer.

'Tired, my lord,' she said quietly. 'I am tired.'

Was this her way of showing her displeasure at his behaviour earlier? Was this a wife's way of responding to something she did not like? 'My lord?'

'And my courses came today,' she added, not meeting his gaze.

He stepped back, wondering what that meant to them. 'Are you in pain? Do you need Leoma to fetch a potion or something to ease your discomfort?'

She shook her head, still not looking at him, and walked to the bed. 'I think I just need to rest.'

'Then seek your rest, Gillian. You did not need to await my return first.'

She winced then and he wondered if he'd offered some insult to her. But he looked down and noticed that she clasped her wrist in her hand. Brice reached down and lifted her hand closer. Signs of a nasty bruise already marred the skin there.

'How did you injure your wrist?'

She pulled it back, but she cradled it against herself. 'I stumbled, my lord. I put my hand out to brace myself and fell against it.'

His bad day just got much worse; he knew now that he had hurt her with his coldness earlier, but worse still, she was lying to him now.

It took but a moment's look at her wrist to see the mark of a hand around it. Someone's harsh grasp had caused her injury. Someone bigger and stronger and someone bold enough to lay hands on his wife. But how could Oremund, for he was sure it was her brother, have been here and none of his men know of it?

Brice turned and looked at the wall. He took a step towards it, but was stopped by Gillian's voice.

'I do not feel well and would seek my bed, if you would allow it?' she pleaded.

Accepting it for the diversion it was, Brice nodded, his heart heavy now with suspicion. 'Do you need assistance?'

'Nay, my lord. Just some rest.'

He stood nearer the door, aching to go to her, aching to beg her for the truth, but not daring to move. She unlaced her over-tunic and pulled it free as she approached the bed. Instead of turning her back and asking for his help in removing the gown beneath it, she climbed on to the bed, favouring her good wrist as she moved.

'I can help you with your gown,' he offered.

'Nay, my lord,' she said, shaking her head. 'I am chilled and the extra layer should help to warm me.'

Because you will not be beside me to do it.

He heard the words she did not speak, telling him clearly that he was not welcome in her bed. Between the 'my lords' and the rejection of his help, Brice knew he would sleep alone this night. Worse than his absence from her bed was that, when given the chance to explain, she'd chosen to lie to him.

'Sleep well, then, lady,' he said as she settled in the middle of the bed.

With her back to the wall.

He did not realise what bothered him until much later, after returning to the hall and being the centre of jesting as the other married men welcomed him into their ranks. Between commiserating about finding himself sleeping alone after only a month of marriage and thinking about her expressions and her actions, Brice finally understood the situation better.

Gillian's courses were simply a convenient diversion to keep him at bay. Though he'd initially put some distance between them with his actions, she feared letting him close now.

Something else had happened in that chamber. Someone had hurt her. But she did not trust him enough yet to share it with him.

After eating and tarrying a bit longer, he returned to the bed-chamber he'd first claimed when they arrived and where he'd slept that first week. It was cold, dark and it held no memories of his wife. He tossed and turned in the large, empty bed for a few hours before realising he could not sleep without her. Finally giving up the fight, he walked down the hallway to her room.

Brice entered quietly and stood by her bed, watching her sleep for a few moments. He smiled when he heard her arguing with someone in her sleep for it seemed to be her custom and he often listened in on her part of the discussion in her dreams. Thankfully, it was not the night terrors that had struck those times during the fever, when no amount of soothing or cajoling could keep her from believing her death, at Oremund's hands, was approaching.

She shifted then, moving and spreading out her hand as though looking for something. Gillian had moved aside, leaving room for him now and he decided that he was unwilling to sleep alone. He pulled off his clothes and slid in beside her, pleased when she turned into his embrace without hesitation. She might be caught in the grip of sleep, but there in this bed, she trusted him.

Holding her in his arms, listening as she spoke her mind to someone else, Brice comprehended the basis for her lack of trust. Everyone in whom she'd placed it had failed her and unless she protected or planned or escaped on her own, there was no one she could count on to be at her back.

Her mother and father, through no fault of their own but in death, left her defenceless against her brother's machinations. He suspected that her mother's death had broken the old thane's heart and his will to live and he could not see past his pain to make arrangements that would keep his daughter safe. Especially in the face of Oremund's defection and support for Eoforwic's hereditary enemies in the north.

A betrothal and marriage would have protected her. But her father was controlled by grief and missed the opportunity to do that.

Her father's most serious failing, other than backing the wrong king, was his disregard for his son. Oh, Brice had no doubt Eoforwic had his reasons, but by ignoring the situation brewing in his estates and with his only son, her father had brought about his own downfall and hers.

Well, nearly hers. He smiled then and kissed the top of her head. His arrival had stopped that just as he would stop Oremund's plan, whatever it was.

But first she must learn to trust him.

He knew just how to take the first step and he would begin on the morrow. She might not have friends and comrades as he had the other bastards to guard her back, but he would be hers. With that decided, Brice closed his eyes and began to let sleep overtake him.

'Brice.' She said it as though a sigh.

'I am here,' he whispered back. 'I did not wish to sleep alone.'

'I am glad of it,' she said, snuggling closer to him. 'I am glad.'

He slept deeply then and woke in the morning with a new resolve about his wife and how he could gain her trust. When the sleeve of her gown slipped and he saw the darkening bruise in the shape of a man's grip around her wrist, he knew there was not much time.

Chapter Sixteen

'Walk with me.'

Gillian looked up from her work, sorting through piles of fabric they'd discovered in a trunk, and found her husband staring her with intent eyes. At first, they appeared to be black, but then the darkest brown showed as he tilted his head to her. The women with whom she worked lowered their heads, but not before she saw the knowing smiles on their faces.

'Worry not, lady,' Leoma said. 'We can continue with this until you return.'

She stood and took his hand, allowing him to lead her to wherever it was he wanted. Instead of heading towards her bedchamber, he walked out through the hall and into the yard. Gillian knew that he slowed his pace so she could keep up with him. She'd seen the way his long legs ate up the distance across the yard when he was in a hurry.

Soon, they reached the door to the guard tower and he allowed her to go ahead of him as they climbed to the top. Brice reached over her to push open the heavy metal door for her and they stepped out on to the highest place in the keep. After dismissing the guards on duty, he brought her nearer to the edge.

'I am planning to enlarge the walls of Thaxted and would have your counsel on some of it,' he said, holding out a scroll to her.

Gillian knew that there was more underway than simple repairs, for most of those had been accomplished within the first fortnight after his arrival. Opening the parchment, she examined the drawings there and smiled. Her father had spoken about doing some of these same things—enlarging the area surrounded by the wall, bringing the cottages of the freemen within, building a stable and a separate stone kitchen.

'You would move the wall out here?' she asked, pointing to the place on the sketch and then to the place they could see.

'Aye. And this could be your own garden, if you wish, for growing what you wish,' he said. 'Such as...' He paused as though trying to think of something to grow. 'I confess I do not know what kinds of things ladies like to grow in their gardens!' He laughed aloud then.

'Have you never been in a garden before?' she asked.

'For certain I have,' he said, nodding his head. The slight change in his skin—a blush?—told her his visits to gardens had nothing to do with herbs, vegetables or other growing things. Unless she included desire.

'And what have you seen there?' she could not help but ask.

'Moonlight. A beautiful woman. Her angry husband,' he said. 'Mayhap we should not have a garden after all?'

'I would love a garden,' she said. 'Over there, here...' she pointed to the drawing again '...by this part of the wall where the sun's light will be strongest during the morning hours.'

'Just so, then, you shall have your garden,' he agreed.

* * *

They spent the next hour or so discussing his plans, changing them according to her suggestions and arguing about several items. Amazingly, he might have lapsed into his habit of cursing in the Breton tongue, but he never discounted or ignored her advice.

Lucais and Stephen joined them and continued to offer corrections or additions for making the keep itself stronger and for improving its defences. She only realised later that they expected further attacks and had already implemented a number of changes without her knowledge to protect them all.

Much of the morning had passed before they finished and Gillian was filled with elation and accomplishment by her involvement in the future of Thaxted.

Something her brother would never have bothered doing.

Something her husband had, despite whatever misunderstanding they'd had the day before.

He made it clear to her and to his men that he valued her opinion and her wishes.

'Why did you do that?' she asked after Lucais and Stephen left them.

He stared at her for a moment and then off in the distance as though trying to decide what to say.

'I think that you have been on your own too much, forced to rely on yourself to see to your protection, forced to hide your intelligence, forced to flee when things became too dangerous. And through all of this, you have been on your own with no one to depend upon.' He smiled and took her hand, rubbing it as he continued.

'I have been blessed with constant friends and companions who have always watched my back—in battle and in life. They have counselled me, advised and harassed me and, most importantly, I think, rolled me into a safe corner when I drank too much and could not make it back to my bed.'

She laughed then, wanting to meet these 'bastards' who had played such an important part in making her husband the man he was today. A man she was certain she could…

'I also was fostered and raised by a man of sense and wisdom. I can still hear his words,' he explained. Then he stopped and stared off again.

Lord Gautier had fostered the three bastard sons of other noblemen, raising them along with his own legitimate one. Gillian had heard this part of Brice's story from others.

'I have always thought I did not have family, but now, considering the parts they have played in my life, I see that I do indeed have one.' Tears burned in her eyes as she noticed their glint in his. 'Now, I wish to have my own family. With you. And with children if we are so blessed, Gillian.'

He lifted her hand to his mouth and kissed it gently. 'I want to show you that you can trust others—you have just not had the chance yet. I want you to be part of this, not standing outside looking on as I build a future, our future.'

She wanted to accept his offer. Her heart wanted him as much as her body did, but she could not give in yet. He was right—every time she trusted in someone they betrayed that trust. Whether apurpose or through no fault of their own, she was left time and time again to fend for herself. And once she'd gained confidence in her own mind and thoughts and actions, it was difficult to acquiesce to another, to lay it all before them and allow them to take control of her life.

Though now, learning about him as she had and seeing how he lived his life and the ideals he upheld, she wanted to. For the first time since her mother's death and her father's decline, she wanted to give it over into someone else's hands.

'I wish I could have the time to show you I can be counted on in good and bad times, but I do not. We do not,' he said. 'Though your brother does not proclaim it openly, he is in league with those who seek to rebel against the king. Even now he shores up support for Edmund Haroldson. This holding, your little Thaxted, lies in the crossroads that are necessary to launch an invasion into lands under William's rule.'

'Thaxted?' She had never been farther away than the convent, so she had no idea of the importance of her holding—a piss-hole, as Oremund had called it.

'Edmund has been gaining allies in Wales, and though the northern earls and Edgar the Atheling are in Normandy with William, their network of spies and those who do their bidding are at work even now to smooth his way. Your brother is in league with all of them.'

Now Oremund's need for the gold made sense. It was not about his inheritance, it was about buying a place among these lords who would use it to overthrow King William. She had no love for this Norman king, but she suspected that Oremund looked only for power, no matter who held it, nor the cost of it.

'I must return to my duties now,' he said, easing a step away from her.

'I will think on your words.' She promised the only thing she could right now, as too many strong emotions, fears and memories swirled inside her mind and her heart.

He began to turn to leave, but she grabbed his hand then, wanting to clarify what was happening between them, trusting him a bit by revealing one of her fears to him. It was not much, but she forced herself to do it.

'What happened yesterday? Between us?' she asked. When he frowned, she was tempted to forget about asking. But she needed to know and to understand. 'Do you not want me any more?'

He surprised her then, lifting the front of his chainmail shirt and placing her hand over his very large hardness. She would have pulled away, but he held her hand there, letting her feel his shape and size.

'I want you so much that it hurts to breathe, Gillian. I want you every moment of each day and, sometimes, I can think of nothing else than filling your body with mine again and again until we cannot breathe or speak or think.'

She was breathless now, from the memories of how he made her feel, of how he had filled her time and time again until they could not move, of how much she wanted him, as well. He released her hand and rearranged his shirt.

'Yesterday, I realised that there is much more I want from you than the use of your body. I want your mind and your spirit, your soul even.' He smiled that wicked smile then, the one that made her want to peel off anything she was wearing and beg him to kiss and lick his way up and down her body. 'Oh, I want that, too,' he said as though reading her thoughts. 'But the rest is even more important and I realised that we were no closer in purpose than when I found you on the road to the convent.'

He leaned in and kissed her then and she tasted and felt all the same passion as before. It had not dwindled or disappeared at all, it just lay banked as a night's fire was, waiting to burst forth.

'I but await your word that you are…ready and you will find my desire for you is still there.'

She let out her breath and tried to calm her racing heart. He nodded to her and began walking down the stairs. She decided to enjoy the cool breezes of the day before going back to her work. But, by the time she saw him come out the door at the bottom of the stairs, Gillian knew she must trust him.

'Brice!' she called out his name. Then once more when he did not seem to hear her. 'Brice!'

She turned and ran down to catch him before he left. She was out of breath when she reached the bottom of the stairway and ran past the guards about to take up their positions at the top again. Brice caught her in his arms and waited for her to be able to speak.

'Brice, he was here last night. Oremund was here,' she said. Clutching his arms, she explained, 'I am sorry I did not tell you.'

'Was he alone? When did he come? Where?' Brice asked in rapid succession. He called out to Stephen and Lucais and then waited on the rest of her words.

'I do not know if he was alone. He was in my chambers when I returned there to wait for you after supper,' she said. 'He left when you and your men arrived back in the keep.'

He drew her into his arms and just held her for a moment. She'd taken a larger step than she probably realised in admitting the truth to him. But now he would ask her to take a larger one still.

'Where does the tunnel lead?' he asked, releasing her from his embrace so he could listen.

'From my chamber to the smithy.'

The blacksmith again. Her uncle. Could he be in league with Oremund? 'Come, I want to talk with your uncle.'

They walked across the yard towards the small cottage that Haefen used as his smithy. He noticed that her hand slipped into his and she clutched it as they walked side by side. Though she might not have noticed, he did and it touched his heart to know she was trying to trust in him.

The shutters that would be opened to let in the breezes and light were closed and locked. Stephen banged on the door but there was no sound within. Without much effort, they broke down the door and went inside. Brice waited, standing between Gillian and the smithy. Stephen came back out.

''Tis empty, Brice. He's not here,' he reported.

'Ask around. Find him.' Stephen went off to investigate and Brice led her inside.

''Tis over here, in this corner,' she said, leading him through the orderly cottage to the back.

'Nothing looks amiss. His tools are here.' Brice glanced around and saw no signs of struggle in the confined area. 'Where does the tunnel open?'

As he watched, she pulled what looked like a cabinet open to reveal a small, metal door. Reaching up to the left corner, she slipped two fingers into an opening and slid them up, down, then up again. The seemingly solid wall moved under her touch, opening to reveal a dark tunnel behind it.

'Now close it.'

She nodded and he watched as she did, using a slot in the opposite corner to move the door closed. Gillian stepped back and let him move closer. Though his understanding of wives was lacking, he understood locks and mechanical devices. He'd learned during part of his disreputable past, before being gathered in by Lord Gautier. Being able to pick or disable locks had come in handy many times in the past.

Calling to Lucais, he searched for a torch and lit it from the smith's coals. After giving orders to return Gillian to her chambers and with Ernaut summoned and at his back, Brice stepped into the narrow passage and began to follow the twisted path along until he reached the small stairway cut out through the stone wall. But before he climbed the steps, he searched for other branches and found two, each one hidden behind another doorway.

They were ingenious devices, for the builders hid the doors and mechanisms well, and they were easy to use, so that even a woman could manage if she knew about them. As he crept on through them, he noticed signs of damage along some of the ground stones. As though someone had been searching for something other than doorways. Digging for something?

Brice climbed the stairs and came to the end. From the position, he suspected he faced the wall in Gillian's room and when he reached up and found the mechanism, the wall opened and he found her standing there, clenching her hands and looking very worried.

'I was going to open it and come searching for you. It took you a long time,' she said. She stepped aside to allow him and then Ernaut to exit from the cramped space.

Brice pulled the door and let it close, watching the way it swung. A counterweight moved it smoothly. Impressive. He could not help but admire the skill needed to design and implement such a system.

'Your father had it put in?' he asked as he let the door close.

'Aye, when I was born—he became obsessed with an escape route in case of trouble.'

'Wise. An excellent system,' he said, dismissing Ernaut with a warning not to speak of it with anyone but Lucais or Stephen. 'Did you know that someone has been digging in the tunnel?'

'No.' She shook her head. 'I have never stopped to look when I used it.'

He laughed then at her disgruntled expression. 'It is not a place that makes one wish to stay within it. Do you use a torch?'

'I have never had time to get one and take it.'

Of course not. If forced to use the tunnel, she was running for her life and did not look left or right, up or down. 'Did your father show you the path of it?'

'Nay. He told me the path. Down the steps. Turn right. Take twenty-five paces and turn right again. He showed me how to release the door.'

So, she had no idea of the other tunnels branching off the main one. But he suspected that Oremund did.

'Can you lock it so no one can use it?' she asked.

'Do you think he will come back?'

The question hung out there for a moment and only a slight nod gave him her answer. Brice looked around the chamber. These devices were usually made with a key that could interfere with the locking mechanism, making it impossible to release the counterweight.

'Did your father give you any keys after your mother died?' he asked. Hiding something in plain sight was sometimes the craftiest way to keep them guarded.

'Only the household keys,' she said, reaching down to the ring that hung from the girdle at her waist. 'These.' She released the catch and held them out to him.

Brice took them and walked nearer to the window to examine them. Four of the keys were similar in structure and caught his attention. He recognised the design and took them from the ring.

'Those are for...' She paused as she looked at them. 'I do not know what those are for. I thought you might have added them to the ring since coming here.'

'When did you last see these? Before my arrival?' He was seeing more strands of that web now, more connections between Oremund and Eoforwic's death. 'Think carefully, Gillian.'

'Before my father left with King Harold. Then again when Oremund arrived here with news of his death. He carried the keys to show me his authority.'

Brice placed the four similar keys on the stone floor in front of the brazier and took out his dagger. After lining the tip of it up with a line down the centre of one key, he shoved the dagger down as hard as he could. As he thought would happen, the key split in two. He handed them to Gillian with instructions to keep each set together and he repeated the action, splitting each key into two pieces.

'How did you learn something like that?'

He laughed at her expression, not certain if she was horrified or proud. When he was done, he took each set and tried each key separately into the notch in the stone next to the door. When he found the one that fit, he placed it inside the mechanism and tried to open the door. It did not move.

'And how did you learn that?'

'I was not always the fine, noble man who married you, Gillian,' he began. She laughed then, and it sounded good to hear it, in spite of the seriousness of the situation. 'At one time, in my headstrong youth, I lived among a gang of thieves and made my living by stealing. I learned all about locks, how to make them and especially how to open them.' He nodded at her disbelieving look. 'There was not a door I could not open or a lock that could keep me in or out.'

'Lord Gautier knew?'

'He suspected.' Brice smiled then. 'At the very least, I would have lost a hand as punishment if I'd been caught, so the first thing he did when he summoned me was to tie my right hand behind my back so it was useless. He left me that way for three days and nights and then asked if that was how I wanted to live.'

'A smart man.'

'Aye, without a word, I learned that lesson quickly. Learning about honour took a bit longer,' he confessed. 'Though I rarely use the skills I learned, I still have them.'

'What do you plan to do with those?' She looked at the other keys.

'I do not want to lock these completely. If I do, you will have no way out if you need to escape. But, I can set them so that you can enter here...' he nodded at the closed wall '...and exit below in the smithy.'

'I do not want him able to get in here again, Brice,' she said, leaving no doubt about her feelings on the matter. 'Close it— seal it if you have to in order to keep him out.'

They were interrupted before he could explain the rest to her. Stephen called through the door to him. Tempted to speak to him down in the hall, he realised that though it would most likely reinforce Gillian's fear of trust, she must know the truth for herself.

'Did you find him, Stephen?'

The warrior glanced from him to the lady and back again. 'There is no sign of him. My men searched every place in the keep and the yard and buildings. No one can remember seeing him after the evening meal, after your return to the keep, Brice. He is gone.'

'My uncle?' she asked, walking closer to Stephen. 'He would not leave Thaxted.'

Brice did not say a word—he did not have to. His wife might be emotional, but she was intelligent and she was putting the pieces together for herself. He watched as the truth hit her and her hands shook. Then all colour left her face and, when she faced him, the bleakness in her gaze hurt to see.

'He would not,' she said, shaking her head. Her mind might be seeing the truth, but her heart fought it. 'He protected me. He helped me escape. He would not...' She did not finish, but only stood there, denying it to herself.

'Go, keep searching,' Brice ordered.

'He is not here,' Stephen argued.

With a nod of his head, he dismissed the man, his best hunter. And if Stephen could not find him, there was no doubt in Brice's mind that Haefen was gone.

The only question was how deep into Oremund's plans was he and what was his price for his co-operation.

Chapter Seventeen

A storm was brewing.

She could feel it, in her bones and in her heart. Gillian moved through the next sennight without much thought. She carried out her duties; the ones that had offered such joy to her at first she now did by rote. When her courses finished, Brice joined with her again, but even that was tainted now by the pain of her uncle's bitter betrayal.

Morning came, the day passed and night arrived. Again and again, without much meaning or importance to her. The only way she could make it through each one was to block off her feelings and not allow the horrid pain too close. Now that her last link to her mother and father was broken, she convinced herself that she felt nothing.

Tension within the keep and people of Thaxted grew, winding tighter and tighter, until she knew something had to break. Brice's men continued to train and to build and rebuild, hoping that the new wall would keep out the danger. But Gillian knew it was impossible. For when evil men are determined, not much can stop them.

When the attacks began in a circular pattern around Thaxted

and Brice was forced to send out troops of men to deal with each one, trying to catch the ones behind it, Gillian noticed the pattern before Brice did. He was too busy trying to hold all the pieces together while fighting a seemingly invisible enemy.

Now that she'd lost everyone dear to her, he stood to lose the most. If he failed to hold Thaxted for his king, he lost his lands, his title, and even possibly his life. And, she'd overheard at some point, that the last of the three bastards, Soren, would never receive his grant.

But what she feared most about telling him the rest of it was that he would change and become like Oremund. Men killed for it. Men were blinded by the promise of gold. Men became drunk and obsessed trying to possess it. Gillian feared seeing the expression in his eyes when he wanted the gold more than he wanted her.

And in the dark of the night, before the storms arrived, Gillian knew the truth. She did have something else to lose. Wrapped in his strong embrace, one that never faltered through the worst of nights, she realised that this Breton knight had managed to get past her defences and burrow deep into her heart. And if Oremund succeeded in destroying him and his dreams, Gillian could neither forgive nor live with herself.

For that would be losing the last person in the world she loved. And, if she loved him, she must trust him with the whole of it.

She woke with a sense of purpose that had been missing for weeks and asked to join him when he met with his men that morning. When everyone had broken their fast and most went off to see to their duties, he kept her at his side.

'Lady Gillian has asked to speak to us,' he began. She could see the puzzled expressions of the men seated around the table in the corner.

'My brother believes that there is a hoard of gold somewhere in Thaxted.' She stated it plainly and boldly. 'And he believes I know where it is.'

The one called Richier let out a long whistle. 'That explains much.'

'And is there this hoard of gold?' Brice asked quietly. She would not meet his gaze, unwilling as she was to see him want something more than he wanted her.

'My father promised Thaxted to my mother and told us there would be gold enough to support it if he was gone,' she said. 'That much I know. The rest is all rumour and conjecture.'

'Part of the morgengabe, lady?' Lucais asked.

She looked at him. 'Aye. So that she would have no claim, no reason to claim his other estates and wealth.' He nodded his understanding of how things were done with wives not sanctioned by the Church.

'And this gold? Where is it?' Brice asked.

So it would begin. She knew if she met his gaze, the hunger there would not be for her. Her heart hurt, so she avoided his eyes.

'After my mother's death, he never mentioned it again. I do not know if he ever had it or planned to use it to go to war against Tostig and Hardrada. Or if he gave it to King Harold.' She shrugged. 'I know not.'

'Oremund believes it,' Brice said. 'He believes you can lead him to it.' All the men looked at him and he shook his head. ''Tis why he kept you alive, Gillian. Why he killed those around you—to force the truth from you.' His voice softened. 'Why he had you beaten and starved.'

The other men at the table gasped and growled then, as one, and now stared at her. It was curious in a way that these burly, strong, ruthless warriors were bothered by her brother's actions. What was a little torture if it brought results? She glanced towards Brice.

'He still believes it's here. He needs it and will do what he must to find it.'

'Then we must find it first and let him know we have it,' Brice stated. She began to argue that it was not here, but he shook his head and smiled at his men, who all smiled back at him and then laughed. Had they lost their wits? As she watched them, she decided there must be some secret language spoken only among men who fight together, for with a glance, a shrug, a nod, a shake of their heads and a few guttural curses, they seemed to have an entire plan formulated in minutes.

Brice ordered them to meet back at the evening meal when all was in place and stood as they left. Now that they planned their own search, she did not want to see the lust for it in his eyes. Gillian stood as well and turned to go back to the kitchen, but he stopped her with a hand on her arm.

'I want to thank you for doing that, Gillian,' he said softly.

'For telling you my brother's motives? You should be angry with me not telling you sooner.' She finally dared to meet his gaze, steeling herself for what she would find there.

His eyes darkened then, but not with lust, not for the gold or for her. They darkened and something else shone in their depths. Something she could not believe she was seeing there.

'Not about your brother or the gold, Gillian. For finally trusting me with the truth.' His voice lowered then. 'For taking that step and trusting me with your secrets.'

He stepped closer, wrapped his arm around her and bent down to kiss her. He'd kissed her dozens, nay, hundreds or even thousands of times since taking her as wife, but none of them matched this one. It was as different from the ones before as every one after this would be. It marked a change between them and she felt it in her blood, in her heart and in her soul. His mouth touched hers and a promise was made between them.

And when he lifted his mouth from hers, Gillian looked into his eyes to see if she'd been mistaken. But she'd been right, for love stared back at her.

'I must go, but wait for me this night,' he said as he stepped away as Stephen called out his name.

She could do nothing but nod, for tears threatened and her throat grew tight. He walked away then, but turned back twice before he reached the doorway to the yard. Then when he did reach it, he cursed aloud and said something else to Stephen. Turning around, he returned to her and pulled her into his arms, so tightly she nearly could not breathe.

And the kiss!

This kiss was filled with fire and heat, desire and wanting, promises and love and it took her breath away with its power. He touched his lips to her and possessed her mouth, tasting, caressing, and making her whole body ache for more. Then, as quickly as he'd begun, it was over and he ran to catch up with Stephen.

Gillian felt more in that moment than she had in the weeks before and a new sense of anticipation filled her. Not only about the night ahead, but also about the possibilities of defeating her brother's aims and living without his interference and threats.

And all because she had finally decided to risk trusting Brice.

The entire keep seemed to come alive that day, awaking from its slumber and working together for one purpose. Gillian found there was joy in accomplishing her household tasks and watched as everyone who could did something.

Outside, she knew Brice was putting some plan in motion, one that involved the gold. And Stephen, who'd spent weeks searching for her brother and her uncle, now turned his skills towards finding the gold. No matter that it could not be here in Thaxted, no matter if it existed or did not.

The hours crept by for her and night would not come. Staying busy should have helped, but it did not. Working with her hands did not. And watching the women as they smiled knowingly made it even worse. Finally, the sun dropped down in the sky and those in the keep prepared for night.

And she waited in her chambers for Brice.

He was certain he knew what had caused her to take the step, but, regardless of the reason, he was pleased she had. Trusting him meant more than even the love he saw in her eyes—it meant their very survival.

The information she provided showed Brice the reasons for the growing web surrounding Thaxted and gave him options he did not have before. His men understood immediately because, in that instant of revelation, they went from being victimised to being powerful.

She'd given them a weapon and there was nothing a man-of-war liked better than a good weapon. Gillian had freed them from their position of watchfulness to one of action. All because she finally trusted him.

The love was something he never hoped for and so was even more special to him.

Brice spent the day in planning and working to use what they now knew to defeat their enemies. And though it meant destroying Oremund and Gillian's true last link to her family, he would do what was necessary to safeguard their future.

All through the day, while thoughts of Gillian swirled in his mind, something else nudged at him. Something about her father's true plan to protect his wife and daughter. Something about the gold. When he finally climbed the steps to her chambers, all thoughts of that part of the puzzle fled for all he could think about was loving Gillian.

He knocked and then pushed the door open.

Gillian stood before the brazier in only her shift. The low light given by it was enough to outline her womanly curves through the thin fabric. He could see the dark pink tips of her breasts, already pebbled and tight, and that enticing triangle of curls between her legs. As he moved closer, she turned to him and smiled, one that would have tempted him, if he'd been Adam, to give up paradise, but this one promised it to him.

When he would have kissed her, she ducked away, taking him by the hand and leading him to the side of the bed. Without a word, she began to loosen the laces at his neck and pulled his tunic over his head. Then she worked on the belt and did not seem surprised when his erection burst out as she pushed his braies down from his hips. She reached out towards it and he waited…waited for her touch.

She laughed and shook her head. 'Not yet,' she whispered. He did not want to wait and shuddered in anticipation of it.

She pushed him back to sit on the bed and if her hand slid over him by accident, she laughed it off.

His chest grew tight and he could not draw in a breath then, as she knelt down between his legs and removed the leather garters that held his leggings in place and then his boots. She was too close. Too close. Heat filled his blood and the need for her pounded through his body. Gillian laid her hands on his thighs and caressed him, sliding her fingers back and forth from his knees to his… Hell, she stopped again just before intimately touching him.

Brice could not be certain if he growled or begged in that moment, but she finally slid her hands forwards and touched him there. With her fingers massaging him, she teased him and taunted him with the promise of it. He dragged in a ragged breath and prepared for the almost-painful pleasure of her caress. When her touch was with her lips and not her hands, he fell back on to the bed believing he had died and found paradise.

He leaned his head up and watched her moving up and down on his shaft, her mouth tight around its width and her tongue tasting him as she moved. Her loosened hair fell over his legs and he reached out to grasp it as she suckled on him. He grew harder and larger in her intimate kiss, but she did not slow her attentions. He wrapped his fists in the length of her hair, holding her close and guiding her pace.

Then his release was coming, his shaft shook and tightened in her grasp as she milked him of every drop of his seed. The tremors moved through his body as he shuddered with it. Gillian did not slow her pace and had not taken her gaze from his; even now she watched every second of his pleasure until he fell back, his body satisfied and his heart full.

The best part was that she was not done. He watched now as she stood and climbed up on the bed and over him, kissing her way up his thighs, across and over his belly on to his stomach. Her kisses and the touch of her tongue made the muscles there ripple and she continued up on to his chest, her hair trailing along tickling his skin with its softness. By the time she reached his own flat nipples, and praise heaven she moved slowly in her pursuit, he was ready again.

He used all his strength to do nothing, enjoying every touch, every kiss, and every caress by her fingers and lips and tongue and not wanting it to end. But now he wanted to show her the desire, the wanting, the yearning and the love that filled his heart for her.

Though not as experienced as other women might be, Gillian could tell the moment he let go. From the way his body trembled beneath her fingers and her mouth, she knew he enjoyed her attentions and fought to let her continue. He pulsed like something alive in her mouth, making her own body shake with pleasure. And despite using her mouth on him before, she'd never brought him to release there.

His growl was the only warning she got, for a moment later she was on the bed and he moved over her like a storm, all power and fury and sensation until she begged and begged for completion.

And he ignored her pleas.

Her body arched, it shook, it trembled, it grew hot. Her nipples tightened, her muscles clenched, her core wept for him.

And still he denied her that last moment.

When she tried to move faster or harder, he stopped.

When she lay compliant beneath him, he began again until

she could not breathe or think or do anything but feel the pleasure of him. There was not an inch of her that he did not kiss
or suckle or bite and caress. He moved her as he wanted. He
touched her as he wanted. He loved her as she wanted.

Then, in one shocking instant, as he plunged in so deep he
touched her womb, she found the first release and shuddered
and trembled over and over in his arms. By the time he was
ready to spill his seed, he'd forced her back to that same, earth-
shaking edge with his strong, deep penetrations and the touch
of his mouth and hands.

They shattered together this time, and it was difficult for
Gillian to know where his body ended and hers began. And
for a short time, she could not tell, as they breathed as one,
moved as one, peaked as one.

He kissed her then, as the waves continued to move through
and over them, and again and again until her body ached for
more. He slid out of her and rolled onto his side, keeping her
in his embrace. A long time passed before either of them could
speak.

When he could gather his thoughts, for they had scattered
at the first touch of her mouth on him, Brice considered what
pieces of this puzzle he might be missing. Holding her close,
he untangled her hair as he thought about the possibility that
a treasure did exist.

If her father had set aside gold for her mother's use, he would
have told her where it was. What good was something if the
person needing it did not know its whereabouts? Then, at her
mother's death, Eoforwic would have told Gillian. If the old
thane ignored his legal wife, his legitimate son and other es-

tates, whether he was besotted, ensorcelled or controlled by Gillian's mother, someone must know where the gold was.

'Gillian,' he said softly, trying to rouse his wife from her exhausted slumber. Instead, she snuggled closer, making him smile with masculine pride. 'Gillian, sweet, wake up.'

Brice watched as her eyes opened, then she met his gaze and her body shuddered with some vestige of leftover pleasure. 'Brice,' she whispered.

He smoothed her hair out of her face. 'When I asked you if your father had ever given you keys, you said no. Did he ever give you anything else? A gift, mayhap? Jewellery?' he asked.

He could tell the moment she came fully awake. 'A necklace. He gave my mother and me matching necklaces.'

'Do you have it still?' he asked. Knowing Oremund's ways, he suspected her brother took everything of value from her.

'Aye. I sewed it into the hem of my cloak to keep it from Oremund. I had forgotten about it until now.' She raised her head and rested it on her hand. 'Is it important?'

'It might be. If your father did have gold hidden away for your use, he would know Oremund would want it.'

Brice did not want to get her hopes up when there was really no proof that it existed. He had enough to support Thaxted and they would be all right without this supposed gold, but Brice thought that the knowledge that her mother and father had tried to protect her interests and future would go a long way in helping her to heal.

'Do you have your mother's necklace, as well?'

She did not answer right away, but then she shook her head as her eyes filled with sadness. 'Nay. My father said she was buried with it in the convent.'

The words struck him as peculiar. 'He said what?'

'He told me that everything he held dear in life, other than me, was buried in the convent.'

Luckily he had tired her and she was too sleepy to realise a possible interpretation to those words. But he did.

He needed to see the necklace to see if what he thought was possible. As he turned onto his side and curled up behind Gillian, his mind began to swirl with plans and possibilities. By the time the sun rose the next morn, he'd barely shut his eyes. There was much to do before Oremund's return and little time, if his informants were correct, to do it.

Chapter Eighteen

Brice waited at the top of the guard tower for Gillian to arrive. The day was clear and bright and the weather improved over the storms of the last few days. But that did not mean rain would not strike tomorrow.

Since that day a week ago when Gillian revealed about the hoard of gold for which Oremund searched, he'd put his plan in place. It involved many of his men, his fighting forces as well as those who worked in the keep and in the fields. It involved understanding the greed of men, the motivations of those who rebelled and how one man's attempt to protect the woman he loved had spiralled out of control. In many ways it could be said about him, but in this case it was about Gillian's father.

Now, in just a few minutes, his plan would go into motion and everything would move forwards. Unfortunately in love and war there were other variables that one could not control, and sometimes things did not work out the way they were planned. He hoped that would not be the case here in Thaxted. He heard her chatting with one of the guards, laughing even, before he saw her. Then she burst through the door and brightened his heart in ways he'd never dreamt possible.

Once she spied him, her eyes were for no one else and it warmed him. They'd come a far way from the night he'd caught her and she'd knocked him unconscious.

'My lord,' she said, 'you called for me?'

'I did, my lady.' He looked behind her and waited a moment. 'Where is Ernaut?' The two were summoned at the same time.

'He said he will be in a few minutes. Finishing up some task or another, my lord,' the one guard offered.

Brice dismissed them and took Gillian's hand. Leading her around to the other side, where they could look down on the yard, he smiled at her. 'What should we do to occupy ourselves while we wait on young Ernaut?'

She launched herself into his arms without hesitation and they spent the next few minutes in amorous pursuits, something he'd never thought possible with a wife. By the time Ernaut arrived, her circlet was knocked askew, her veil lay in a twist around her neck and her lips showed every sign of being kissed, and kissed well.

'My lord.'

'My lady.'

'My lord!' Ernaut called out from the doorway trying to get his attention.

Brice released Gillian, who smoothed her hair down, replaced her veil and positioned the circlet where it would actually hold the veil before facing the boy. But it was the way she licked her lips that nearly drove him back into her arms.

'I have serious matters to discuss with both of you,' he began, lowering his voice by habit. 'Gillian, I need your co-operation. Ernaut, you must be my lady's fiercest guard and see to her protection. If I do not know, for a fact, that both of you can follow my orders without question and without delay, I cannot go forwards.'

He watched her think about his words, wanting her apprised of the plan. She was not stubborn, actually; once she understood something and comprehended her part in it, she presented some of the best analysis of plans and procedures he'd seen. 'The attack, when it comes, will be of life-and-death importance to all of us, so delay or hesitation will cost lives. I cannot fight and give my complete focus to battle when I am worrying about the safety of my wife.'

Her eyes filled with tears then and, if not for Ernaut's presence, he would have taken her in his arms and tried to soothe her fears. The boy cleared his throat as though he knew Brice's thoughts.

'Ernaut.' He looked at the young man who had proven himself ready for such a task. 'At the first sounds of trouble, whether battle cry or attack, seek out Lady Gillian and become her personal guard. You must help her in her task and do only that. Do not become engaged in the battle. Do not be waylaid by others' calls or needs. You are to see to my lady only.'

'Very well, my lord.' Ernaut nodded crisply.

'But what is my task, my lord?' Gillian interrupted.

'My love, I want you to do what you do best,' he explained, but the look in her eyes spoke of something completely different from what he meant now! 'I want you to run away.'

'Your pardon, my lord?' Her gaze narrowed on him. 'Run away?'

'You must get out of Thaxted and get to the convent as quickly as possible. Ernaut will cover you and protect you, but I know you will help, as well.'

'Run away?' she said, clearly aggrieved at his praise for her skill.

'Not everyone could extricate themselves from dangerous situations, Gillian, and get away from their foes,' he said as an explanation. 'Granted you've not managed to escape from me, but you did escape from your brother several times.' He glanced from one to the other. 'I need you to do it again and get to the convent safely.'

Before he could say anything else, the cries went up in the yard and word spread. One of the guards came running up to tell them.

'They found the gold, my lord. Stephen found the gold!'

Ernaut yelled out and Brice sent him off to have a look. Gillian looked shocked, but he kept her at his side and the younger man ran down the steps and towards the corner of the keep.

'There is no gold here in Thaxted,' she said simply and clearly when Ernaut was gone.

'No, Gillian, there is no gold in Thaxted.'

At that moment several of the soldiers carried out a dirty wooden chest, the lid of which was opened, revealing a large gold cross and chain on top. Everyone in the yard ran to see it as they carried it past into the keep. When they cheered and looked up at him, he raised his arm and cheered along. Turning back, he faced a grim wife.

'Then what, pray thee, was that?' she asked, crossing her arms over her chest and narrowing her eyes at him again.

He said nothing, giving her a few moments to work out his plan on her own. Her gasp told him she understood.

'You bait a trap here?' she asked. 'You draw Oremund to you?'

'And Edmund Haroldson, as well,' he explained. 'And some of their northern allies who should legally be observing the truce William issued when he took their earls to Normandy.'

'Brice, this is too dangerous.' She reached out and touched his arm. 'We do not have enough men, enough weapons, to fight off such a force as theirs.'

'Aye, we do, Gillian. When all my forces are gathered in one place and not spread out fighting this group here, and that group there.' He motioned off in the distance where the recent small attacks had been.

She seemed lost in thought for a few moments, looking around the yard and out towards the fields, now planted with spring crops. Her lower lip trembled, but then she met his gaze.

'I want you to crush him under your boots for what he has done to my father and to Thaxted.'

A chill ran down his spine and for that moment he was glad she spoke of someone else and not him.

'I will,' he said, gathering her close. 'But I can only do that if I know you are safe. You must promise me that you will get yourself to the convent when the attack occurs. Immediately. Without hesitation or question.'

'I promise, Brice.'

He kissed the top of her head and stepped away. 'Only Stephen, Lucais and a few others know the gold is false. Ernaut does not.' Offering his hand, he guided her to the steps. 'Come, let us look on the treasure of Thaxted.'

She laughed and in that moment, Brice realised he was looking at the treasure of Thaxted—the only one that mattered to him.

* * *

'What is the news from Thaxted?' Oremund demanded. He knew the informant had arrived at their camp, but had not yet presented himself to Oremund. His men looked one to the other, but no one answered his question. 'Where is he?'

'He comes now, my lord,' someone called out from nearby.

The informant, the same one who'd told him of his father's escape tunnels, approached, followed by Edmund and the two men on whose lands they hid and who served Earl Edwin. Haefen stepped nearer.

'They found the gold.'

Oremund felt his blood begin to boil and the air before him began to sparkle in front of his eyes. That lying, thieving bitch! The scream poured out before he could control it.

'I will cut out her lying tongue before I slice her throat,' he yelled out, letting his rage flow. 'She's known all along and she tells that Breton bastard where it is?' He looked at her uncle. 'And you did not know? You told me there was no gold at Thaxted. What say you now, Haefen?'

The smith said nothing then. A wise decision for the stupid peasant. Gillian had let his wife die instead of giving up the gold to Oremund. Let him stew on that for a while!

'Edmund, gather our forces. We march on Thaxted,' he ordered.

The planning went on through most of the night and by morning, they knew how they would take Thaxted. And though Oremund still seethed over his whore sister's deception, he knew that, within days, the gold, Thaxted and she would be under his control and her Breton husband would be worms' meat.

That made him smile.

And he'd not smiled about anything in a long time.

* * *

Gillian would have laughed if not warned before when she looked at the chest filled with gold. The top piece, the one that drew your eye, was real, but the rest was not. Though gazing around the hall at the people, she knew that most of them would not have ever seen real gold in their lives, so it mattered not.

And according to her husband's plans, by the time Oremund got close enough to tell, it would be too late.

Not soon enough, she decided, feeling an absolute and unforgivable thirst for his blood to be spilled. For his sins—all of them.

After allowing everyone to see the gold, Brice had it locked and chained and placed in the storeroom with a guard in front of it. All for show. All to gain Oremund's attention. Brice's plan would work because Oremund would not be able to resist the temptation to come back for the gold. And to punish her. And to kill Brice for his part, too.

As she watched the preparations, she prayed that her uncle was not part of this. She was at peace knowing that Oremund had to die, but she knew that part of her would die if Brice had to kill Haefen. Watching Oremund kill his wife must have turned him somehow, she was certain. She just could not believe he would betray her. Could not.

That was the only sadness in this new life she'd found since being captured by her Breton husband. Her uncle had been a good man, a dependable man, a happy man, until Oremund tore their lives apart.

The days filled with work, but her nights were filled with passion. Brice held her close and they whispered about their future, about their pasts and their plans. And when she closed her eyes each night, she prayed for such things.

She'd almost thought that Brice could be wrong about the possibility of attack after several days of waiting showed no sign of it. Then, when she dared hope that Oremund would not fall for the bait, the call came.

The walls had been breached and Oremund was on the attack.

Chapter Nineteen

Smoke filled the yard as the attackers set fire to anything that would burn. Rage filled him for the moment, but he let that go. Brice knew it would happen and knew that he could replace and rebuild. But it was the people he wanted protected.

And they were. As ordered, they followed his men into the tunnels to wait out the fight. It removed innocents out of his men's sights and would save more than if they ran.

He saw the guard's signal from the tower and knew that Oremund's men were coming from the north, as they had suspected. With the southern approaches clear, Gillian should have no difficulty getting away.

If she followed his orders.

He fought his way towards the gate, allowing Oremund's men to swarm into the keep, searching, he knew, for the chest of gold. He would owe Father Henry for that cross and the chain if Oremund managed to actually get away with it. Though his men appeared to be unprepared and off-guard, they followed Stephen and Richier's plan to perfection and soon herded Oremund and Edmund back out of the gates.

Then, finally, pray God, he saw Gillian under Ernaut's

protection as they crept along the wall to the opening he'd made there. She turned back twice, but then she pulled her cloak over her head and followed Ernaut. Once he knew she was on her way to safety, he fought as he wanted to, going after the men who would destroy all he loved. A short time passed and the guard gave another signal.

Word spread through the yard that Gillian had escaped and it rippled out to their attackers. He heard Oremund scream above the battle sounds the moment he learned it. His first thought would be to go after her, so Brice threw his men in to block his path. He would slow Oremund down and give time for Gillian to reach the convent.

Brice used his sword on another soldier and swung his mace at another, falling into his battle rhythm of sword, step, mace, step over and over again as he rid himself of those who attacked him. He watched with grim pleasure as his bowmen, standing in the tower and along the stone sections of the wall, picked off more. With the battle in constant movement, Oremund could not set up a stand of archers to hem his men in and he watched as they flowed out into the fields around Thaxted Keep.

It would take her only a short time to reach the convent; the trained destrier that waited for Gillian and Ernaut had stamina and strength and would cover more ground than most could, even with two on his back.

The sanctity of the convent would not protect Gillian from her brother, nor would its walls, but Brice had arranged for something that would.

He wished he could be there to see Oremund's face. But his job was to clear Thaxted of invaders and then bring up the back of the lines to keep them from escaping north. Oremund would fight no more after this day and Edmund Haroldson would be where he should have been put months ago during the fight for Taerford—in the ground just as his father was.

Gillian wrapped her arms around Ernaut and leaned low against his back as they flew down the road. At this speed, they would reach the convent walls soon. The horse beneath her showed no signs of slowing or being winded as they raced south away from Thaxted.

She did not want to run. She wanted to stay and fight with her husband, but she knew he was right. She would be a distraction, and as he'd told her again and again, distraction meant death in war. So Gillian leaned against Ernaut and prayed as she never had for the safety of her people…and her husband.

They passed by the field at the top of the rise just before the convent where Brice's first camp had been. No sign other than impressions on the ground remained behind to mark the spot where she'd met him for the first time. Just when the convent should come into sight, she felt the horse slowing.

'Nay, Ernaut,' she cried out. 'Brice said go to the convent. Do not stop.'

Still, the boy pulled in the mighty warhorse under control and slowed him to a stop. 'My lady,' he said, breathing heavily from the exertion.

Gillian peered around him to find a mass of mounted knights between them and the convent walls. And the first line of archers stood with bows aimed at them.

'Lady Gillian, I presume,' the knight in the centre called out.

Though Ernaut tried to keep her on the horse, she slid off and walked towards the knight. Ernaut could not hold the destrier and her, so he dropped the reins of the horse and positioned himself between her and the archers. When the horse began to run off, a shrill whistle from the second knight calmed it. The horse followed the whistle to the knight who dismounted and took the reins.

'Stay back, my lady,' Ernaut pleaded, drawing his sword and brandishing it before them.

'You and your lady are in no danger from us, boy,' the taller knight called out.

'I am Giles of Taerford, Lady Gillian,' the first knight said as he approached, lifting his helmet so that Ernaut could identify him. 'This is Soren, also friend to your lord husband.'

Giles motioned to Soren to remove his helmet, but the warrior ignored him. Gillian doubted that Soren did anything anyone told him to do. Ernaut finally recognised Brice's friends and put his sword away.

'Here, boy,' Soren said, bringing the horse back to them. 'You must take her to the convent.' Soren, taller almost than the huge warhorse, gave Ernaut a hand up and then lifted her in one smooth motion up behind him.

Gillian had questions to ask Lord Giles, but was given no time. Within minutes, she was safe within the convent's walls with close to one hundred mounted knights, archers and soldiers between her and her brother's men.

And her husband's. If he yet survived.

When Oremund and his cavalry chased off after Gillian, Lucais's troop and the archers on the walls made quick work of the foot soldiers left behind. Stephen and Richier came out of the forest with their horses, kept out of sight of the attackers and readied for their use. Already fewer than half of Oremund's force remained while Brice had suffered few loses.

With the control of Thaxted clearly back in his hands, he called out orders to those remaining behind and took his knights towards the convent.

They rode as though the devil followed them. For his plan to work, he must catch Oremund's forces between Giles's and his and squeeze them in between. He filled the miles with prayers—prayers for her safety—and soon they approached the fighting. Looking ahead, he could see Giles's formation and Oremund's men trapped now between.

He smiled grimly and placed his helm back on. God help them all!

Though Edmund tried to warn him from following his sister, Oremund would have none of it. The chest of gold at the keep had been a ruse, to draw them in, but his sister's escape told him that the real treasure was at the convent.

He realised as he rode that his father would have sent anything of value to be hidden on the convent grounds. The Reverend Mother was the late king's half-sister and so the convent had always been well guarded. Now, though, he would find what his father left behind and it would be his.

Gold enough to buy more soldiers to fight against the Norman invaders and their Breton lackeys. Gold enough to be taken seriously by the northern earls. Gold enough to sustain him and his titles.

Gold enough for the respect he deserved.

Following the road, with his men at his back, he came over the last hill before the convent and could not believe his eyes.

A wall of men—nay, three different walls—stood between him and everything he fought for. A row of dozens of archers knelt in front. Another row, two deep, of foot soldiers with a row of mounted knights at their backs. All with weapons at the ready, arrows nocked, all waiting for the word.

One knight rode forwards and asked for his surrender. The knight called out the demand first in French and then in heavily accented English. Oremund spat on the ground in reply.

Edmund whispered furiously behind him, but Oremund did not hear his words. He could see the convent walls behind them and knew that was his true target. But he needed to survive to break through and for that he needed his men in front. Riding back, he ordered his men into lines, knowing that the first flight of arrows would get many of them. It did not matter—they were expendable, he was not.

The cry to battle rang out and the arrows flew. Men and horses screamed as they hit their targets. Oremund circled back around his men, far enough to avoid the arrows, searching for a way through. As the Normans began to move forwards, a small opening occurred as several of the knights dropped back behind the others. Edmund called out orders for a retreat, which Oremund countermanded. Confusion reigned as the soldiers did not know who to follow or which way to go.

Oremund used the chaos to get nearer to the road. When his horse was slain from under him, he managed to untangle himself and rolled along the ground. Edmund was in command now and called out, directing the fight. Unfortunately, any advantage they might have had was gone.

When another battle cry rang out behind them and they saw the Breton from Thaxted's approach, their men panicked and ran in all directions. The knights ahead of them were loosed and the field became a slaughter.

But, Oremund would not give up.

Not now.

Not this close.

Brice saw Oremund's forces being decimated before him. With no reinforcements possible, he watched as Giles first used his archers to thin the ranks. Though his friend had enough arrows and time to sit and pick off every one of those caught between them, Brice knew his friend was eager for battle. When Brice saw Edmund race off the field to escape, Giles gave the order that released his men and they covered the field, a killing force that could not be stopped.

Giles, followed by another knight, rode after Edmund. Dear God, could it be Soren? Brice shielded his eyes from the sun, but they were into the forest before he could be certain. It was then he spied Oremund sneaking along the edge of the forest, making his way towards the convent.

Brice spurred his horse on, racing across the field, through the fighting men, trying to get to Oremund before he found a horse on which to escape or, worse yet, to reach the convent. Then, just as Brice reached the road and thought he would get to Oremund to stop him, another man came out of the shadows of the forest between them.

Without hesitation, Haefen swung the heavy mace, catching Oremund in the leg and knocking him to the ground. As he lay there writhing in anguish and unable to get away, the smith brought the mace down again, hitting Oremund in the chest and throat. Brice looked away when the third blow was struck, but understood Haefen's need to do it. When Brice looked back, Haefen dropped the mace and spat on the dead man.

Brice rode over now and climbed off his horse. Haefen nodded at him.

'For my wife,' he said sombrely.

'And for mine,' Brice added, holding out his hand to Gillian's uncle.

His man Stephen had discovered that Haefen was actually following Oremund and began collecting reports for Brice about Gillian's brother's plans. But Brice could not share that truth with Gillian. 'She thinks you betrayed her. The truth of your actions will ease her heart, I think.'

With their leader's death, those still fighting scattered. Brice gave orders to chase them down and kill any they caught, knowing that alive these men would simply find new leaders and come back to haunt him. He'd learned from Giles's error in judgement in allowing Edmund to live and would not make the same mistake. Of course, his lady wanted Oremund dead, where Giles's had not wanted Edmund to die.

He waited as his men took control before going to her. Though he wanted nothing more than to hold her in his arms, there were tasks to see to before his personal desires. As he was speaking to Richier, Giles rode back onto the field. And indeed, it was Soren at his back. They approached and dismounted and he greeted them warmly.

Giles tossed his helm to his squire and embraced Brice.

'That Edmund must have magical skills, for he disappears better than any I know.'

'If you had killed him as I suggested—' Brice began, but Giles waved him off.

'I know, I know.' He laughed. 'You were right.'

Brice turned to their friend and waited for him to come closer. As Soren began to lift off his helm, Brice felt Giles squeeze his arm, as though in warning. Even so, Brice did gasp when Soren turned to face him.

The left half of his face was the same as it had been, the appearance that got him called 'the beautiful bastard', but the right side… Dear God! Though healed, it was a mangled mess of skin and scars, and his right eye was gone. Brice tried not to stare, but such damage was horrifying. Finally, he reached out to Soren and took his hand, pulling him into a rough hug.

'And what does the other knight look like?' he asked, trying to ease the tension between the three of them.

'He burns in hell, Brice.'

'I am glad of it.' And he was. 'My thanks to you both for coming in my time of need,' he said. 'How is Lady Fayth?'

Giles sighed dramatically. 'Women are not very logical when they are carrying. She cries at everything.'

'So this was no hardship for you, then? Coming now?'

'Oh, *non*! You may have saved my life by calling me to your side,' he said, laughing. 'You will see what I mean.'

'Did you meet her?' he asked. 'My wife, Gillian?' Brice realised that the field was under control and he could go to her now. 'Come with me?'

They mounted and rode to the convent wall, where Ernaut greeted them with the news that Gillian was safely within. As they left their horses with him and walked inside, Brice felt the anticipation of seeing her again, of knowing that the threat to their happiness and their future was gone now. The other two laughed at him as he nearly ran to the heavy door and knocked on it.

They laughed louder when he cursed the slowness of someone to answer it. And when he began to pace. Finally, several minutes later, an old woman, an old nun, tugged the door of the gates open and asked his business as though she did not know his wife was inside while a battle raged without! He tried to adapt his pace to hers as she meandered along the path that would take them to the Reverend Mother's public chamber, but Brice found himself wanting to pick up the holy woman and carry her along faster.

When they finally reached it and Brice was informed his wife awaited him within, he rushed past her and opened the door.

The room was empty.

There was no sign of Gillian.

His shout shook the chamber and echoed through the corridors and rooms of the holy convent, scaring the pigeons on their roosts and the nuns at prayer who now believed they were under attack.

Brice leaned his head back and called her name out as loudly as he could. Where the hell could she be?

Chapter Twenty

Ernaut handed her down when they reached the gate and waited for someone to escort her in. He assured her, in his earnest way that he would guard the entrance, and her, with his life if need be. She did not have the heart to tell him that four mounted knights sat in the shadows of the road for that purpose.

It had been difficult to ignore the sounds behind her as she walked into the enclosure, for she knew men were dying because of her. When the Reverend Mother allowed her to use her own public chambers, Gillian began by praying. Kneeling on the floor, head bowed, she tried to erase the sounds of killing and dying that echoed over the wall and into her thoughts.

Was Brice hurt? Had her brother followed as they'd expected? Was he dead? How many of their people had perished? Was Thaxted burned to the ground? Her worries grew, adding another question to her list as each moment passed.

Gillian paced then, walking the length and width of the chamber and then again and again until she grew dizzy. When she could stand waiting no more, she pulled open the door and looked down the long corridor for anyone who could tell her where the Reverend Mother was.

Creeping along, trying not to disturb anyone at prayer, Gillian peeked inside rooms until she reached the end of the hallway. Opening the last door, she discovered she now looked into the graveyard. She'd not been here in almost a year. Her mother's grave sat in the far left corner, under an arch of flowers and growing vines that her father had built in her memory.

Gillian walked to it and knelt down next to the grave. The stone read 'Aeldra, Beloved of Eoforwic' and it brought tears to her eyes when she realised that her mother rested here alone. Oremund said he'd been unable to claim Father's body after the battle, so she had no idea where he rested now.

Did the dead hear the living when they spoke at their graveside? Could her mother hear her words? So much had happened since her last visit; as Gillian knelt there, it all poured out of her.

Father's death. Oremund's violence. Brice's arrival. How they'd fallen in love. His plans to see her and their people safe. Gillian talked and talked, sharing her feelings with her mother as though she could hear her. She ended it with an official prayer in case that made a difference. Then she leaned back on her heels and waited for some sign that her mother had heard her.

The bellowing sounded like a wounded animal…

Or an angry husband!

Gillian climbed to her feet and brushed the dirt from her cyrtel. She heard him shout out her name again and then he burst through the door, striding through the graveyard until he stood before her. His two friends, a growing group of nuns led by one angry Reverend Mother and a few of the lay women who lived and worked with the sisters surrounded them.

'I thought…' he whispered as he stopped before her. 'I thought…'

Then he said nothing but pulled her into his embrace and kissed the breath out of her. She allowed it because it felt so good to be in his arms, but then realised where they were and leaned back.

As she looked at him, she noticed the cut above his eye, a bruise on his jaw and other small injuries. She touched his face gently and then began to cry as she realised he was alive.

'Oremund?' she asked through the tears.

'Dead,' he said, while his two friends spat on the ground.

'Edmund?'

'Escaped,' Brice said.

'Again,' Lord Giles added.

She could not bear to ask the next question, but he knew what she wanted to know.

'Your uncle lives, Gillian. He awaits you outside.'

'What?' She was shocked by his calm announcement of such news.

'He has been working with us against Oremund and did not betray you as you feared.'

She cried harder then, not sure if she could believe such a happy ending to what could have been such a tragedy for all of them. She felt him hold her close and soothe her with soft, whispered words until she regained control. He released her and she stepped to his side. One last thing and they could go home.

'Would you say a prayer with me at my mother's grave, my lord?' she asked quietly. It felt right to ask him, so his response was a surprise.

'Gillian, your mother is not dead.'

Had he lost his wits? Had he been injured and struck his head and was now confused? 'My lord, she died here six years ago.'

He turned her to face him, took her hands and shook his head. 'Your mother is not dead.'

'Brice, 'tis not something to jest about,' she warned. Pointing to the grave at their feet, she said, 'She lies right here.'

He turned and looked at the group of nuns watching this absurd scene and met the eyes of one. Gillian followed his gaze and noticed the sister standing a bit farther away than the others. The good sister was crying, probably in shock at this situation. But then she raised her eyes to Gillian and she recognised those eyes in an instant.

Dear God, her mother was alive. Her mother was alive!

Brice had considered letting the lie remain in place, but Gillian deserved to understand why her parents had chosen the path they had. She had paid such a price for it; she deserved at least the truth. Thinking back on some of Gillian's comments about her mother's ties to the convent had sent him here searching for answers. So he watched the nuns around them as Gillian spoke and quickly noticed the one who stood alone, watching and listening to everything that happened, but never once raising her eyes. When something startled her and she did, he saw the same turquoise eyes as his wife's and knew he was right. Lady Aeldra of Thaxted yet lived.

Though tempted to expose her, Brice waited, hoping that she would approach her daughter with the truth. Exhausted from having nearly lost everything and everyone that mattered to him, he had paused for a moment before revealing the shocking fact and Gillian had recognised her mother with one look.

Now, as she crumbled before him, he was not so certain he'd made the correct choice. He reached out and took hold of her before she fell, lifting her into his arms and carrying her to a bench nearby. Sitting down and holding her on his lap, he waited for her mother to approach. After the Reverend Mother spoke to her and then asked the others to leave, Lady Aeldra walked over to them.

'How did you know?' she asked softly, reaching out to touch Gillian's face and then stopping just before she did.

'Something Gillian said. The truth was there, but she was too young to understand it when it happened.'

'She will not understand it now,' the lady replied. 'I did it to protect her, to protect Eoforwic.'

'She will be hurt, but I think not knowing is worse. She grieves for your loss still and she deserves to learn the truth from you, from her mother.' Brice watched as Lady Aeldra reached out to touch Gillian's face again.

'I have grieved the loss of her as well, my lord.'

Brice felt the pain in her words and knew her actions had been done for the best of reasons—she loved her daughter and tried to protect her.

'Speak to your daughter, then. Make her understand,' he pleaded softly. His own heart lightened at her nod. He wanted Gillian happy now that she was safe. This was the first step.

Gillian began to stir in his arms and opened her eyes. 'Brice? I had the strangest dream. We were at the convent…' Her words drifted off as she realised it was not a dream at all. 'Mother? Is it really you?'

Lady Aeldra opened her arms to Gillian and Brice watched as Gillian was held by the mother she had thought she'd lost.

Gillian sobbed and Brice found it difficult to observe without being affected. He stood and moved away, giving mother and daughter a chance to talk.

Giles and Soren stood nearby and he walked over to speak with them, but he had to clear his throat several times before he could get any words out.

'So, the lady has been here all the time?' Giles asked.

'Apparently so. I suspect that she thought her death would stop the escalation between Gillian's father and her brother. She was willing to give up her daughter to protect her.'

Brice glanced over at Soren, who now wore a black hood over his head, so that much of the damage to his face was covered. Fashioned after the chain coif that protected their heads, his was made of leather. Another leather patch lay strapped in place and covered where his eye should have been. Soren noticed his curiosity and walked away.

'Is he in pain?' Brice asked of Giles.

'He says not, but I suspect he feels much that he does not say.' Giles let out a breath. 'He is very changed from the friend we knew.'

'How could he not be? He faced death and came out alive.'

'I do think he believes he was not lucky in living, not with all he has lost.'

Brice shook his head, not understanding such a thing, but Soren's good looks were a part of him, now gone for ever and he faced constant scorn and fear over what he had become. ''Twill take time, Giles.'

'I think it will take more than time for him to find the man who has always lived beneath his skin,' Giles replied.

Brice turned back to Gillian and found the two women

sitting now on the bench, talking quietly. It would also take some time for them to be reconciled and for Gillian to understand why her mother chose to leave her.

He walked over to them and offered Gillian some time with her mother before returning to Thaxted. Though she declined at first, he could tell she wanted to stay, so he convinced her that it was a good thing to do.

Giles and Soren planned to set up camp just over the hill, so he knew she would be safe here while he saw to repairs back in Thaxted. He would have her for the rest of their lives, so he felt that he could be generous in giving her mother a few days of that time.

Before he would leave, though, he wanted the feel of her in his arms for just a few minutes, so he held out his hand to her and she took it without hesitation. Taking a few steps away, he lifted her face and kissed her gently. The tracks of her tears still glistened on her cheeks and he thought she would cry more before she was done. Sharing truth could be a most difficult thing for both people involved, but he was glad he'd revealed what he had to his wife.

'Do you forgive me for not telling you sooner?' he asked quietly. She was precious to him and he hated thinking that she would not forgive him for the secrets about Lady Aeldra and about her uncle that he'd kept. Gillian smiled and his heart lightened at the sight of it.

'All this time I have felt alone and all this time I had protectors I knew not of—my mother, my uncle. My husband,' she whispered as she reached up and kissed him.

When he found that he was tempted to do more than just kiss her, he let her go and turned to leave. Lady Aeldra's question stopped him.

'Do you not want to know about the treasure of Thaxted, Lord Brice?' she asked.

He turned back and smiled, glancing from one set of blue-green eyes to the other. 'I have the treasure of Thaxted, lady. I have no need to seek it out.'

He'd realised long ago that what Oremund thought his father protected was not gold. 'Just as Eoforwic thought you the thing most important in his life, Gillian is that treasured thing in mine.'

He fought off the soft feelings that came from such an admission, but accepted his words as the truth. He'd been given something more valuable than gold. He had a wife to live with him, to care for him and to love him all the days of their lives when he never thought such things could be his. His bastard friends, the only family he'd once known, would now be part of the family he and Gillian would create now.

Brice left them then, following Giles and Soren to set up their camp.

A few hours later, he and Ernaut rode back to Thaxted, where he arrived to cheers. His men seemed in good shape, those injured already cared for, his dead being buried first and repairs underway to the wooden structures that had been burned in the attack.

As he walked through the keep, around the yard and other buildings, he felt a sense of gratitude that they'd been able to save so many and so much.

He slept that night only because he was exhausted, but he did not like it. Even in the worst of times, he liked having Gillian in his arms.

* * *

So, if he was in a hurry the next day to claim her back from her mother and the convent, it was understandable to any sane person. Brice rode past Giles and Soren, waving off their invitation, and made it to the convent in the shortest amount of time possible.

Part of him worried that she would want to stay with her mother now that she'd found her. To make up for the lost years. Part of him wondered if she would truly be happier there, for that had been her destination when he captured her. And part of him just worried.

So when he opened the door into the Reverend Mother's public chamber and she ran into his arms, he let out the breath he did not know he held in. The Reverend Mother was there and did not look very happy, though Lady Aeldra smiled at him.

As they rode back to Thaxted, Gillian explained, and all he could do was laugh. While he was worrying that she would find appeal in the contemplative life, she was breaking the rules and speaking during their meals! It was obvious to all that Gillian took great delight in the joys of marriage. Then she had tried to convince her mother to renounce the vows she took and come to live at Thaxted.

Though she was always welcome to visit her mother, the Reverend Mother suggested clearly that once a year would be the acceptable frequency for such visits. Brice had laughed so hard, he nearly knocked them both off the horse. Though indignant over his reaction, it took less than an hour once they were together in bed to show her four other things she would miss if she lived in the convent, or even if she visited there too often. By the time she'd climaxed for that fourth time, Gillian finally agreed to give up the idea for ever.

Chapter Twenty-One

Thaxted Keep, northeastern England
July 1067

Brice looked out from the guard tower and smiled. In the bright summer sun, his fields blossomed with life and prosperity. Lucais predicted a huge, successful crop and already had plans to expand the number and layout of the fields for next summer.

With the threat gone, Giles returned to Taerford for the birth of his first child and he had made Gillian promise to come and meet his wife. He told her that they would have much to commiserate about since they were both strong Saxon women married to Breton men.

And Soren…Soren was a changed, haunted man searching for a way to live after having come so close to death. There was a dangerous anger seething through him and Brice worried for him. When Bishop Obert arrived, there had been some contest of wills between the two of them over the king's grant—Soren wanting to head off on his quest of vengeance while the bishop had another task for him first. Ultimately, Soren rode north to secure the rest of Eoforwic's lands before they were swallowed up by the northern earls.

Obert shared Brice's concern for those two who seemed to be puppet masters yet, but mostly Brice worried about uncontrolled darkness seeping into Soren and his need for vengeance. They'd learned long ago that battle was not personal, but Soren had forgotten that lesson after suffering and surviving a brutal attack.

Their plans for improving the keep—rebuilding with stone to replace the mostly wooden structure—would have to wait until Brice had more coins saved, but the wall had been enlarged and expanded as they'd wanted. The rest of the tunnels had been located and filled, leaving only two open for a crisis.

Gillian was reconciled with both her mother and her uncle and had come to understand the reasons behind their actions. He watched her grow in understanding, as the woman she was now comprehended things she could not have as the child she had been when the actions were taken.

In spite of the Reverend Mother's wishes to the contrary, Gillian visited her mother often, sometimes spending the night there. Brice was not happy sleeping alone, but he could see the happiness it brought her. And there was always the time they spent together when she returned to make up for her absence.

Her breasts were definitely larger and the nipples had taken on a much darker hue. As he touched them, circling them with his finger and then suckling them, her reaction was different, as well. She responded to every caress of them more quickly than before.

That was nothing to complain about—indeed, there was much to commend on such a response—but something was different.

When he moved down her body to pleasure her, he noticed that the place between her legs was more sensitive and she arched against his mouth almost as soon as he tasted her essence there. He spread her legs, opening her to his sight and his touch and he saw a difference there in that most intimate of places.

Neither of those concerns bothered him for very long because he was too busy bringing her to a climax. His favourite part was watching her expressive face as she blossomed with the ecstasy they'd learned to find with each other. Well, one of his most favourite parts of it.

She'd been gone for a day and another half and he was ravenous for her by the time she'd returned from visiting her mother. The only thing that comforted him while she was gone was the knowledge that she would give herself to him for hours on end when she arrived back at Thaxted. Now, having her under his touch, to explore and excite and to love, made being a good husband and a godly man worthwhile.

When they'd driven each other mad with desire and satisfaction and they lay entwined in their bed, refusing to leave it until the next morning, Gillian finally laughed over the situation.

'I am not certain if getting aroused is the proper reaction any time I mention visiting my mother at the convent, Brice.'

'How can I stop, my love? You can talk all you want about going and praying, but all I do is walk around hard as stone, waiting and praying for your return. 'Tis your fault, after all—you have trained me to expect you, naked in my bed, each time you leave.' He kissed her then and began to roll over and pull her down next to him.

'Speaking of my mother,' she interrupted.

'I do not think I want you to speak of your mother when you hold me in your hand, Gillian. It is sacrilegious somehow.'

They had let all talk go for a while, but Gillian returned to the subject when they lay ready for sleep in the dark of the night.

'My mother told me that she likes you more because you have not asked about the gold.'

He searched her face for some clue, but found none. 'What gold?'

'The real treasure of Thaxted, Brice. The gold my father left for my support and for Thaxted.'

Brice felt as though he was missing half of some conversation. He sat up, sliding back against the head of the bed. 'I told you and your mother that I have the treasure your father tried to protect. There is no gold and, if there was, I—we—do not need it.'

He dragged his fingers through his hair, which he had allowed to grow longer, and then looked at her. No hint of merriment played in her eyes. Her serious expression made him wonder.

'Does your mother truly think there is gold, Gillian? I truly thought it was simply Oremund's obsession.'

'My mother said there is.'

He thought about it then. At one time, he'd thought that if it existed it might be buried in the grave marked as Aeldra's burial place, but once he accepted that Gillian and her mother were Eoforwic's true treasures, he'd not thought about the possibility of the gold again. Any inkling of interest in it was always stopped when he considered the madness that such a quest had brought about in Oremund. Now, though...

'Does she know where it is?'

Gillian slid over him and off the bed, seeking the small box in which she kept her jewellery and keepsakes. She opened it and brought something to him. When she placed it in his hand, he nodded. 'She instructed me to give these to you and tell you to solve the puzzle.'

'This is the necklace your father gave you.'

'Nay, that is the one for my mother,' she corrected him. 'This is mine.' He took both necklaces she handed to him and held them up before him. Each was a heart-shaped metal necklace with a key at its centre.

'Mother said that you should find the gold so that you can take proper care of her grandchild.'

'I should find the gold,' he muttered, frowning that his wife's mother should be issuing orders from her place in the convent. Then he thought about the rest of what she'd said and stared at her.

'Grandchild?' he asked, whispering the word. 'A child?'

Gillian smiled and nodded as he dropped the jewellery on the table near their bed. He pulled her close and kissed her, still not believing this news. 'When?'

'Mother says near Candlemas Day.'

'And you are well?'

'I grow tired in the afternoon, but that seems to be the

only symptom. And I have missed my courses these last two months.'

That he should have noticed, for it was the only thing that kept them from pleasure. Now that he thought about it, she had not had them but once since they married. But they could discuss the timing of such things later. He just wanted to hold her. She had not said how she felt about it though.

'Are you happy about the child, Gillian?'

'This is what we have prayed for, and planned for, Brice. The family that both of us have dreamt of having.' She touched her lips to his. 'Aye, I am happy to be carrying your child.'

The necklaces were forgotten until the next day when he found them and decided to study them. Taking the ribbons off, he held them up side by side and saw that they were not identical at all, but mirror images.

Days passed and Brice found himself intrigued by the necklaces. The first clue came when he noticed that the key in the centre moved as though hinged on the outer heart-shaped piece of metal. Stiff from years in the same position, he was able to use some oil to lubricate them until they moved easily. Once he did that, he could put the keys together to form a larger one instead of two smaller ones.

He still had no idea of what it could open. Gillian said nothing, only watched as he grew fascinated with the keys.

Then, one day as they worked to repair an older section of the outer wall, some loose stones fell and revealed a memorial plaque for Lady Aeldra. The heavy cast-iron plaque lay fitted into the original wall. Haefen explained that Oremund had become incensed over its presence and when he could not destroy it, he ordered it covered so that he would not need to see it.

It seemed solid under his examination, but Brice noticed a small hole in one corner of it. At first he thought it part of the damage wrought by Oremund until he realised that the key would fit into it.

He laughed at the possibility. Most likely his mother-by-marriage was just teasing him to see if his feelings for her daughter were sincere and his claim of not needing the gold was true. Aye, a test more likely to measure his worth.

Brice had ignored it for several more days, but then decided there was no harm in giving it a try. Early one morning, when most in the keep were still asleep, the timing chosen to avoid looking foolish when it proved nothing, he took the necklaces from Gillian's box and walked quietly to the plaque. He fitted the two pieces together into one key and tried to place it in the hole.

And it fitted perfectly.

As he turned the key, he heard the tumblers rolling and felt a latch let go. The metal plaque released from the wall and a compartment was revealed behind it. A wooden box, half the size of the one that held his clothes, sat inside. When he tried to lift it, the weight of it made that impossible. He would need help. So, he locked it back in and waited until he could bring Lucais or Stephen with him.

Gillian was awake when he returned, but he did not speak of what he'd found until he could bring it to her. After all, it belonged to her. When her mother took her vows, all her earthly possessions went to her daughter and this was part of it. But regardless of ownership, this was her father's attempt to provide for her future and she needed to know how important she had been to Eoforwic.

That night he walked at her side going up to her chambers, anxious to see her reaction. He opened the door for her and she walked inside and then stopped suddenly, not moving.

'What is that?' she asked, shaking her head as though not believing what she saw there.

'It is your mother's gold.'

'My mother's gold? Where did you find it?' She reached out and lifted several coins from the box, looked closely at them and dropping them back inside. 'It is gold,' she said, raking her fingers deep into the box and through the layers and layers of coins.

'Your father left it in plain sight, Gillian. Under the memorial plaque he made for your mother.' He watched as she began to accept that it was real. 'He did not leave you without support. He set this aside for your use. For your mother, for you, for Thaxted.'

He smiled at her surprise, knowing the same expression probably sat on his face when he'd opened the chest and glimpsed the riches within. 'She goaded me into finding it—I suspect she wants us to have it,' he admitted.

'And I know that you will put it to good use, Brice. I trust you.'

Hearing the words that still did not come easily to her, Brice comprehended again how very much she was the treasure of Thaxted.

But the gold would certainly help since there were walls to build and a child to raise. Certainly, the gold would help.

* * *

And so, on the nineteenth day of January, in the Year of Our Lord 1068, a son was born to the lord and lady of Thaxted Keep. His father proclaimed that he would grow into the best man in the world. His mother simply smiled, for she knew that there could be no man better than the one she had married.

* * * * *

Author Note

Although the 1066 invasion of Duke William of Normandy brought about huge changes in the politics and society of England, some of those changes were already underway. Normans had become an integral part of England during Edward the Confessor's reign; many gaining lands and titles long before the Conqueror set foot there. So, the Saxons had some experience with Norman ways before this major invasion force landed in Pevensey in October, 1066.

Many Saxons held their lands after William's arrival—those who pledged their loyalty to the new ruler were permitted to retain them, but many were supplanted by those who'd fought for William. Important Norman nobles gained more property and often Saxon heiresses.

Thought ruthless and not hesitant about using force to implement his rule, William did not employ it fully after the Battle of Hastings until the revolt three years later in the north of England. Then, he unleashed his anger on those in what's still called 'the Harrowing of the North', destroying everything in his path and effectively wiping out what was left of the Saxon way of life.

In my story, one of Harold's sons, Edmund, appears as a leader of the rebels. 'My' Edmund is really a composite of several real people who lived in the aftermath of the Battle of Hastings and continued to fight the Normans as they moved from the southeast of England northward and westward to take control of the whole country.

It is believed that at least two of Harold's sons did survive (or avoid) the battle that killed their father and that they and their mother joined in the efforts of some of the others opposing the Normans. The earls of Mercia and Northumbria, Harold's brothers-by-marriage, switched sides several times during this conflict, were even taken to Normandy along with the designated Saxon heir-apparent, Edgar Atheling, and were later part of this struggle that led to William's Harrowing of the North.

So, any resemblance of 'my' Edmund to the real protagonists of history is intentional!

HISTORICAL

Novels coming in June 2011

RAVISHED BY THE RAKE
Louise Allen

The dashing man Lady Perdita Brooke once knew is now a hardened rake, who does *not* remember their passionate night together…though Dita's determined to remind him! She's holding all the cards—until Alistair reveals the ace up his sleeve!

THE RAKE OF HOLLOWHURST CASTLE
Elizabeth Beacon

Sir Charles Afforde has purchased Hollowhurst Castle; all that's left to possess is its determined and beautiful chatelaine. Roxanne Courland would rather stay a spinster than enter a loveless marriage… But Charles' sensual onslaught is hard to resist!

BOUGHT FOR THE HAREM
Anne Herries

After her capture by corsairs, Lady Harriet Sefton-Jones thinks help has arrived in the form of Lord Kasim. But he has come to purchase Harriet for his master the Caliph! Must Harriet face a life of enslavement, or does Kasim have a plan of his own?

SLAVE PRINCESS
Juliet Landon

For ex-cavalry officer Quintus Tiberius duty *always* comes first. His task to escort the Roman emperor's latest captive should be easy. But one look at Princess Brighid and Quintus wants to put his own desires before everything else…

HISTORICAL

Another exciting novel available this month:

LADY DRUSILLA'S ROAD TO RUIN

Christine Merrill

Mad dash to Gretna!

Considered a spinster, Lady Drusilla Rudney has only one role in life: to chaperon her sister. So when her flighty sibling elopes Dru knows she has to stop her! She employs the help of a fellow travelling companion, who *looks* harmless enough…

Ex-army captain John Hendricks is intrigued by this damsel in distress. Once embroiled with her in a mad dash across England, he discovers that Dru is no simpering woman. Her unconventional ways make him want to forget his gentlemanly conduct…and create a scandal all of their own!

HISTORICAL

Another exciting novel available this month:

GLORY AND THE RAKE
Deborah Simmons

An unsuitable job for a lady!

Miss Glory Sutton has two annoyances in her life. One: the precious spa she's determined to renovate keeps getting damaged by vandals. Two: the arrogant Duke of Westfield—the man assigned to help her find the perpetrators.

Oberon has no interest in this independent, troublesome woman! And Glory couldn't be less interested in the enigmatic rogue!

As they get drawn deeper into the mysteries of the spa, they too must reveal their secrets in order to uncover the truth. And then, perhaps, the legend of the waters will come true!

HISTORICAL

Another exciting novel available this month:

TO MARRY A MATCHMAKER

Michelle Styles

The Matchmaker's Wager

Lady Henrietta Thorndike hides her lonely heart behind playing Cupid—some might accuse her of interfering, but she prefers to think of it as *improving* other people's lives!

But Robert Montemorcy knows it has to stop—his ward has just fled from a compromising situation in London, and the last thing she needs is to be embroiled in Henri's compulsive matchmaking! He bets Henri that she won't be able to resist meddling…only to lose his own heart into the bargain!